When Tornadoes Collide

Laws of Passion, Volume 3

Amara Holt

Published by Amara Holt, 2024.

Copyright © 2024 by Amara Holt

All rights reserved.

No part of this book may be reproduced, distributed, or transmitted in any form or by any means, including photocopying, recording, or other electronic or mechanical methods, without the prior written permission of the author, except in the case of brief quotations in book reviews.

This is a work of fiction. Names, characters, places, and incidents are the product of the author's imagination or are used fictitiously. Any resemblance to actual events, organizations, locales, or persons, living or dead is coincidental and is not intended by the authors.

PROLOGUE

Christopher

"Chris, stop," Anna said in the middle of her laughter, asking me to halt.

"It's only five in the morning; who in their right mind goes out to train at this hour?" I asked, brushing my hand along the side of my wife's face.

"The same person who has little time." Her eyes narrowed with the smile that sparkled on her lips.

"You don't need any of that; you know I can give you the best," I whispered, lowering my face and giving her a lingering kiss on the lips.

"I can't become a future First Lady by being a trophy wife; I need to be an example alongside the greatest man this country has ever seen." It was impossible not to smile at what Anna had said.

"But seven years, that's what I'm missing." I lost myself in my thoughts.

This was my first run for Governor of New York; moving from a California Senator to Governor was easier than I had expected. With Anna by my side, everything felt lighter.

"Are you sure your obstetrician cleared you to be out and about on that motorcycle?" I asked as Anna managed to escape from my arms, walking around our bedroom while her long nightgown dragged on the floor.

"Darling, I'm pregnant, not ill." With a delicate smile, Anna entered our closet.

I let out a long sigh, touched the floor with my feet, and followed her into the closet, where I would once again insist that my stubborn wife stay at home and not go out alone. Or at least sell that motorcycle.

"Anna," I grumbled, stopping at the doorframe.

"No, Christopher, the answer is no." She didn't look in my direction, wearing those *leggings* and a tight shirt over her belly, which didn't yet show the bulge of our growing child.

"Honey, at least accept one of my drivers..."

"Isn't it enough to have that security detail of yours?" She turned her face and tried to win me over with that beautiful smile.

"It's for your own good," I declared as my wife ran her hand through her long black hair, tying it up in a bun.

"You Fitzgeralds are obsessed with control, haven't I mentioned?" Anna shook her head as if what I said didn't matter.

"I just want my wife, and consequently our child, to have the best comfort a person can have, including security." I pointed my finger at her and traced it down to the center of her belly.

My wife walked towards me and stopped in front of me. She was a tall woman, but even though she was tall, she still didn't surpass my height. She held my face on both sides.

"Chris, stay calm; nothing will happen. I'm fine; I'm a great rider. Our baby is doing very well inside me, safe, strong, and healthy." I slid my hand to my wife's flat belly.

"Promise?" I asked, bringing my lips close to hers.

"Yes." I bit her lower lip, pulling it with a bit of force.

"Chris," she whispered amidst a moan.

"Can't you be late?" I controlled myself to avoid being aggressive in my touches. I was holding back from being rude, given my tendency to be somewhat hostile during sex; I was restraining myself from hurting or crossing any limits with Anna.

"Remind me to get pregnant more often, so I don't have to keep asking you to stop," she joked, trying to escape from my arms amidst one of her delightful laughs. "And to answer your question, if I'm late, Ludy will drive me crazy."

Ludy was her personal trainer and also her best friend. They had been training together every morning for at least the last eight years, since we met in college.

"Ludy could understand that your husband is feeling needy." I turned around, watching her grab her phone from the nightstand.

"Needy? You don't know the meaning of the word limit. We've been married for four years, and we haven't reached the phase where we get tired of sex yet," she said with that mischievous look.

"And we never will." I winked playfully.

"Well, soon we'll have a baby in this house; you might get tired of me, of us." Anna bit the corner of her lip.

"No, that will never happen. You are the woman of my life; I knew that from the first glance we exchanged when I saw you on that campus, the most beautiful woman playing volleyball with her friend, Ludy." I rolled my eyes playfully at the mention of her friend's name.

"I know deep down you love Ludy." Anna headed towards the door.

"Of course I love her; she took care of you when I wasn't around..."

"Took care of me? You know I don't need anyone taking care of me," Anna rolled her eyes.

"Yes, I like the image of my wife being cared for." We reached the living room of our house.

"Chris, you and my father should be related. I feel like I'm moving from one castle to another, like a princess." My wife grabbed her jacket from the hook.

"That's simply because you're our princess." Anna stopped in front of the garage door.

I followed her and we shared a quick kiss.

"When you get back from training, I won't be home. Let me know when you're at school," I whispered amidst the kiss.

Anna was a preschool teacher and loved those children. The way she always talked about the little ones was enough to charm anyone.

"Yes, my love," she murmured, opening the garage door and stepping inside.

I hated that motorcycle with all my might. I would have preferred a thousand times over if Anna drove a safer car, but she insisted on saying that she felt free riding that thing.

"I love you, my love." She blew a kiss into the air as she always did, wearing that helmet.

"I love you, my princess." I did the same.

I watched her leave through the rising gate, with my security detail right behind hers. Even with all the barriers I created to ensure Anna's safety, I felt like a failure, as if I was forgetting something. Perhaps it was just my heart that she held in the palm of her hands.

CHAPTER ONE

Hazel

12 years later...

I stopped in front of the mirror, my pencil skirt marking the middle of my thighs, and the buttons of my shirt fastened all the way up. The fabric became loose when I tucked the shirt into the skirt. Since I was ahead of schedule, I slowly did my hair up in a bun.

I left my room, descending the stairs.

When I decided to move to Washington DC at the invitation of Mrs. Natalie Fitzgerald, it was to live in their house. However, I thought it would be too much to ask, considering they were already giving me the opportunity to work in the family law firm, interning and simultaneously acting as Mrs. Natalie's assistant.

My move to this district became even more perfect when Christopher Fitzgerald won the presidential election, bringing with him his vice-president, Zachary Fitzgerald, my brother-in-law, who had just married my sister.

Savannah even wanted me to live with her, but I declined since the two of them were enjoying their first year of marriage and I wasn't going to be the *third wheel*. So I just visit them or help out with Sadie when they need to go to an event. I refuse to leave my niece with anyone else when I can be there, as long as I don't have classes.

But now, with little Alexis, who was born a month ago, my sister and brother-in-law have been staying home more.

5

I never thought I could love anyone as much as I love my nieces.

I grabbed my coat from the hook on the door. It was a bit chilly this time of year, and since I was wearing a thin shirt, I'd easily feel the cold.

I opened the door and stepped outside, feeling the gentle breeze on my face. My red truck was parked in front of the house. I lived in a row of houses, half an hour from the Fitzgeralds' office.

I placed my handbag on the passenger seat and sat behind the wheel. Out of habit, I looked at myself in the mirror, rubbed my lips together, and reapplied my *lip gloss*.

The loud engine roared when I started the truck. I drove carefully down the street, paying attention to everything around me.

I rolled my eyes as I passed by an electronic billboard displaying images automatically, seeing a photo of Christopher Fitzgerald, a handsome man, but bitter, the definition of wasted potential. It was as if he were still married; he even wore his wife's wedding ring on a chain around his neck.

I saw that image during one of his office moments, as always, giving orders. He had subtly leaned down to scold a poor intern, and the necklace slipped out from the top of his shirt, which was unbuttoned at the first button, revealing a delicate ring.

That was the role of the bitter Christopher in the office: just bothering the interns. He paid his attention to the more senior men, as if the lower positions were mere scum in his eyes.

The only reason I exchanged a few words with him was because he was my brother-in-law's cousin and, of course, because I was his mother's assistant.

I drummed my fingers on the steering wheel while romantic music played on the car's sound system. *"Sexed Up by Robbie Williams."* My dreamy side sang along to the melody, imagining the day I would experience a strong, lasting, and possibly very intense love. It wasn't envy, but I wanted something like my sister's relationship, that look Zach had for her, but not from that man, from another man, my man.

I thought that after witnessing so many couples marrying for love and affection around me, I had become demanding, wanting nothing less than devotion.

I believed that the only thing that worked decently in my car was the radio. I couldn't ask too much of my poor truck, which had once belonged to my sister and had been passed down through generations.

I arrived at the parking lot and parked the truck in the back, where it had a small chance of going unnoticed among those luxurious cars.

I grabbed my handbag and got out of my vehicle. My heels echoed on the asphalt of the parking lot as the cloudy weather suggested it might rain soon. I took a deep breath and pushed open the office door, just as my eyes met Emily, the secretary, who lowered her glasses and looked at me from under them.

"Good morning, Arizona girl." I smiled at the nickname they gave me.

At first, I didn't like it much, but I eventually got used to it.

"Good morning, Mimi." Just because of that, I ended up giving nicknames to all the staff.

I held my handbag between my arms and walked to my desk next to Mrs. Natalie's office. I placed the handbag under the desk, removed my coat, and draped it over the chair.

"Good morning, dear." At that moment, Mrs. Natalie arrived.

"Hello, Natalie." I smiled, having gotten used to calling her by her first name after many weeks.

"Give me today's schedule. I have an event to attend and I'm afraid of being late." The woman gave a side smile, elegant and discreet.

Natalie was the epitome of a sophisticated, delicate, and humble woman.

"Yes, I'll take care of it." I sat in the chair, turning on my computer.

My mornings were always very busy. I had many things to deliver to Mrs. Natalie, sometimes attending meetings. Usually, during the afternoons, she would give me some cases to study and draw my conclusions. I liked that job; I might be just an assistant, but Natalie allowed me to be in charge of some of their client contracts.

It was nice to be interning and working in the field I had always dreamed of, even if only partially, since I still had a few years left to complete my course.

It would be very difficult to find my prince on a white horse, especially because I currently enjoyed spending most of my time at the office or at college. I needed to dedicate myself fully to be the first in my family to graduate.

Perhaps, *just perhaps,* it was better that I didn't find any love at the moment, or didn't get distracted by men. My studies would always be more important. Not that I shouldn't enjoy some male company, after all, what would be their best use?

It was good that my prince on a white horse could wait a little longer.

CHAPTER TWO

Hazel

"Did you bring lunch from home?" Ethan leaned over my desk, asking.

"Actually, no." I pouted. "But I'm not the best company today."

"I highly doubt that." Ethan was one of the attorneys at the firm. He was a handsome man, but I didn't want to get involved with anyone from work; nonetheless, he kept making advances toward me.

"Seriously, I have a test at college today; I need to study. Maybe I'll go to the café across the street, get some snacks... coffee." I shrugged my shoulders.

"This college life isn't easy. I believe you could at least go for lunch and then come back. What do you think?" He straightened up, crossing his arms.

"Thanks for the invitation, but I'll pass this time." I winked, shutting down my computer.

"Alright, Arizona girl." He sighed, turning away after realizing he wouldn't get anywhere with me.

I had lunch with Ethan on other occasions. He was good company, but really, I couldn't do it today.

I was bending down to pick up my handbag from the floor when a shadow fell in front of my desk. Slowly, I stood up, knowing I'd find those blue eyes narrowed at me.

"Mr. President, what an honor to have you here." I flashed my most smug smile. I could shrink away and pretend not to know him, like most women did when he was around.

"My mother, I have a meeting with her," Christopher's deep, commanding voice echoed in the room.

"No, you don't." I grabbed my planner from the desk just to confirm that he didn't.

"Yes, I do. Do you think my assistant would make a mistake with my schedule?" His rude tone made it clear that he was losing patience.

"Either your assistant made a mistake or your mother's assistant did, in this case, me. And I don't make mistakes." I opened the planner to today's date, showing him there was nothing scheduled.

The president ran a hand through his hair, as if he could pull it out with force.

"*Hell...*"

"Cursing, Mr. President, I hope your fans don't see you doing that," I teased, closing my planner.

The tall man made a sound that resembled a growl. It was so easy to get Christopher Fitzgerald upset. What he lacked in charm was made up for by his grumpiness.

Being the sister-in-law of his cousin made me somewhat immune to the allure of the most handsome man my eyes had ever seen. Or was it just me being the most daring girl I liked to be?

The office door opened, and Natalie immediately flashed one of her guilty smiles.

"*Oh, God!*" Mrs. Natalie put her hand to her mouth. "It's my fault; I forgot to inform Hazel about our lunch since I need to schedule meetings to see my only son."

She rolled her eyes, judging her son with a look.

"See, dear Mr. President, no one made a mistake." I bent down to grab my handbag from the floor.

"I didn't give you permission to call me that," Christopher whispered, as he always did when I called him that.

"Funny, I thought I had cleared that up in our last meeting," the president growled again.

He knew I only did it to provoke him, or even annoy him. Everything that came out of that man's mouth when he was in the family office were orders and a large amount of ignorance.

However, when he wasn't in the presidency, as a politician, he was impeccable, the best at what he did, even giving small smiles when he wanted to.

Natalie bid me farewell with a smile. Christopher didn't even look my way, no goodbye, nothing. It would have been incredibly strange if he had said goodbye.

I grabbed my handbag and left right after them. I was heading to the café across the street, where there were nice tables for studying, and one of the perks of not living with my mother was not having to worry about what I was going to eat.

Mom had always been very strict; she hated it when we didn't eat well.

I just stuck my foot outside the office, taking in the sight of the exorbitant number of security guards walking alongside the president. I knew it was necessary, but privacy seemed like a distant reality for him.

I hurried across the street, entered the café, and inhaled the delicious aroma of coffee and sweet cake.

Through the glass window, I watched all the *black SUVs* drive away. I sighed deeply, heading to one of the tables, pulling out a chair and sitting down, taking my laptop out of my handbag.

My phone vibrated; I took it out of my bag and saw my sister's name shining on the display. I answered the call and brought the phone to my ear.

"Hazel?" Savannah immediately asked.

"Who else, little sister?" I teased, resting the phone on my shoulder while turning on my laptop.

"You're so funny." I could swear she was rolling her eyes at that moment.

"What's the honor of your call, sis?" My relationship with Sav was always great; we never even fought.

"Are you trying to hang up? As far as I know, it's your lunch break." Savannah replied defensively.

"You're right, it's my lunch break, but I'm a bit busy. I have a test tonight at college." I pursed my lips at that realization; I hated test days, always feeling tense.

"*Oh*, it's nothing major. I just wanted to remind you that this weekend is Zachary's birthday, and I'd like you to be there. It will be just a family dinner, no strangers." Savannah spoke as if I were part of her husband's family.

"Family, you say, just forgot that I'm not actually part of that family. But since I miss my little ones, I'll definitely be there." I smiled, thinking about my nieces.

"There's nothing those two little ones can't do." My sister chuckled softly. "Can I count on you, then?"

"Have I ever missed any of our commitments?"

"Do you really want me to remind you how many times?"

"*Okay, okay*, let's forget those times." I laughed awkwardly.

We ended the call after a lot of discussion about my nieces. I loved talking about them. I placed my order for a strong coffee, as my mom's voice echoed in my mind: "Hazel Bellingham, too much caffeine is bad for you." One of the perks of living alone was not having anyone to restrict me.

If it weren't for the fact that I often felt lonely when I loved talking to everyone around me.

CHAPTER THREE

Hazel

I parked my truck in front of my sister's impressive house. Savannah deserved it for the hard years she spent without Zachary's presence.

I hopped out, smoothing down my denim skirt to make it longer. The short-cowboy-style boots I wore echoed on the path to the house. The door was slightly ajar, so I didn't knock, entering to the sound of laughter coming from inside.

I followed the noise and entered the living room. My gaze met my sister, who was holding little Alexis in her lap.

"Where's my goddaughter?" I opened my arms as Sadie appeared in my line of sight.

"Godmother!!!" With a squeal, she came running towards me.

I knelt on the floor and picked up my goddaughter. I stood up with her in my arms, and Sadie wrapped her legs around my waist.

"*Wow*, what are they feeding you?" I asked playfully.

"A lot of food." Sadie clumsily ran her little hands through her hair.

"Tell your godmother that we're going through a terrible phase where a little lady doesn't want mommy to tie her hair." Savannah came walking towards me with Alexis in her lap.

"Oh yeah?" I made a face at Sadie.

"Godmother, now I'm a big sister." A pout formed on her lip.

"Just forgot the fact that you're still our little baby." I kissed her cheek in an exaggerated motion, eliciting a delightful giggle from Sadie.

When I heard footsteps, I stepped aside towards the corner where Zachary was, without letting go of my goddaughter.

"So you're getting older; the gray hair is already showing." I pointed at his hair casually.

"Cut it out; I looked at every strand this morning." He mocked as he always did.

If all the Fitzgeralds had Zachary's sense of humor, the world would be a much more peaceful place.

I raised my gaze, sensing that distinct smell. Not that other men didn't have their own, but Christopher had an essence that seemed unique to him. Something made just for him, or was it just my dreamy side?

Christopher Fitzgerald was every woman's dream, but his reserved nature pushed away any female interest.

"I'm honored by your presence, cousin." Zachary approached his cousin. The two shared a hug; both were tall, but Christopher was more muscular, perhaps with a broader chest.

"I have a few minutes off." I rolled my eyes at what the president said.

Luckily, my movement went unnoticed. It was strange being in a room with the country's big men, past and present politicians, Zachary's parents were there with Christopher's parents. The only ones missing were William's parents. He was the governor of California and couldn't travel so easily, especially now that Zoey was expecting their first child.

"Godmother, can we go to my room?" Sadie asked with sparkling eyes.

"Of course, do you have new dolls?" I asked, heading towards the stairs.

"Where are you going, sister?" Savannah asked a bit louder, drawing attention to us.

"To play with dolls." I shrugged, smiling.

"I see someone has already managed to kidnap the godmother." Zachary's voice was full of mockery.

"My favorite pastime." I kissed Sadie's cheek, enjoying her sweet scent, as she wrapped her little arms around my neck, hugging me tightly.

I paused at the top of the stairs and let the adults continue their conversation while I followed my little one.

I entered her room, which I already knew where to find. Filled with many dolls, Sadie jumped off my lap and showed me her new dolls. We played together, as my goddaughter made imaginary food, I prepared our daughters for a meal.

We lost track of time. Being with Sadie was pure joy; she might carry the Fitzgerald name, but she had all the spirit of the Bellinghams.

With a knock on the door, I looked up to see my sister standing there.

"I know you're having fun, but how about coming downstairs?" Savannah asked.

"Shall we? Then the godmother will play a bit more." I winked, extending my hand, which Sadie held with her tiny fingers.

The three of us left the room.

"Is Alexis sleeping?" I asked, wanting to know about my younger niece.

"She's with Natalie," Savannah replied.

We reached the first floor, where everyone was gathered, while the president was still present next to Zachary, his father, and his uncle.

"You'd make a great grandmother, Natalie," I said sarcastically, seeing the lady with Savannah's daughter in her lap.

"That's something I've given up hope on." The lady sighed, looking at her son, who at that moment, even from a distance, heard what I had said.

"It looks like a museum stuck in the past." Whenever we were out of the office, I treated them as people who weren't my bosses, just as I was asked.

"Don't get involved where it's none of your business," Christopher said a little louder to make sure I would hear.

"I would doubt very much that someone as cold as you could bring a child into the world, insensitively." I raised an eyebrow.

Our clashes were normal and sometimes ended with long debates. That's because the president was always right, but not in my world; in that world, I was the one in charge.

"Luckily, that's not how a child is conceived," he continued.

"Even if it were, the woman would have to be very brave to want to bring a child into the world." I shrugged and turned my face, making it clear that the conversation was over, and once again, I had won.

Obviously, the woman who had a child with him would be very lucky; I had only said that offhandedly. I had always followed the Fitzgeralds in politics since I was very young and saw pictures of him with his wife. I must have been around 12 years old; my father used to read the newspapers with me by his side, and there was always a photo of him with her. They always seemed very in love.

Out of curiosity, I even searched for photos of her online, and all that could be seen was a loving couple, with a man whose gaze shone with so much love for his wife. Something I no longer saw in him today, that shine and devotion.

CHAPTER FOUR

Christopher

I traced a finger around the rim of my whiskey glass while my eyes were fixed on the baby in my mother's arms. It wasn't supposed to be like this; it was supposed to be my child there. But fate had other plans for me—loneliness was all that was left.

I didn't envy Zachary; I was happy for the family he was building.

Zach was building what I had always wanted for myself. Deep down, I might have harbored a bit of envy. But I couldn't have it all; my chance was gone. I didn't have Anna anymore; she was gone, left me, and it wasn't even her fault.

I knew Mom wanted grandchildren. My parents always said I should give someone else a chance, but how could I do that when no girl could do what she did with me? It was as if Anna had taken my heart with her to the grave.

My eyes wandered to the squeal of Zachary's older daughter. She clearly enjoyed that crazy aunt of hers, perhaps due to the fact that they shared the same neuron.

Okay, it was cruel of me to think that way; it was just a momentary anger towards that woman. Anger wasn't exactly what I felt; I couldn't decipher what it was, but she drove me crazy. A gift that belonged to few, most of the time I would ignore and move on with my life, but not with her. I would retaliate, get out of my mind, and before I knew it, I was already giving back the affront.

"Christopher." I blinked several times, looking at Zachary, who must have been calling me for some time since his voice was strained.

"Yes?" I asked as if I wasn't distracted.

"Is my sister-in-law distracting you?" The bastard caught me red-handed.

"Go to hell, what do you want?" I grumbled.

"It's no shame to admit it; the Bellinghams have a surreal beauty, but one of them is already mine." Zachary took the empty glass from my hand.

"I don't want your wife, let alone her sister," I retorted.

"Obviously, Savannah is mine." He rolled his eyes. "But Hazel would be a woman worthy of being by your side."

"Worthy of driving me crazy, right?" I followed him to the bar, my cousin pouring half a glass of whiskey that he always drank.

"This is not the kind of conversation you're ready for." Zachary handed me the glass. "However, I caught you checking out Hazel."

"It was nothing, I was just wondering how such a charming little creature like your daughter gets along with that crazy woman." I brought the glass to my lips.

"That's a thought unique to you." Zach shrugged.

We returned to the center of the room, and I stood next to my father and my uncle Arnaldo, who was Zachary's father. Arnaldo had been the President of the United States, while my father had been the Governor of California twice and a Senator twice.

When you come from a family of politicians, life ambitions are not much different.

"Did you give poor Sydney a break?" Dad asked with a hint of sarcasm.

"She must be at her house, but always ready to put out any potential fires." Sydney was my assistant, a shadow of mine, always on my tail.

"I know exactly what that's like; only God knows what we'd do without them." Uncle Arnold nodded in agreement.

I grimaced as I watched the girl with the cowboy boots teaching some dance steps to Zach's older daughter. It was hard to take that woman seriously when she was always smiling, making some kind of joke.

Hazel was the typical country woman who, when not in the office, wore one of those so-called *cowgirl* boots, a skirt, and a tight shirt, sometimes with a vest on top. It was as if she had the gift of being two people: the office woman and the one outside. But always a bit crazy.

"No offense, but I think Hazel is too young for you, cousin." I rolled my eyes when I heard Zachary's voice next to me.

"Don't you have anything better to do?" I grumbled.

"Did you see that he was looking at her, or am I going crazy?" Zach looked at the two older men.

"I've given up all hope; I'm convinced I'll have to adopt my siblings' grandchildren," my father said mournfully.

"It wouldn't be that different from William and Zoey," Uncle Arnold added fuel to the fire.

"No, stop this conversation," I wanted to cut the topic as it was taking directions I didn't like.

There was Anna; there would always be Anna. There would be no room for any other woman.

I was saved by the housekeeper who came to announce that dinner was ready; at least I could eat and hide in my house.

Sometimes loneliness was the best companion for broken hearts.

I waited for everyone to be seated, and in that way, I took one of the last available seats. Perhaps I shouldn't have done that because the last seat left was next to her. If I refused to sit next to Hazel, it would imply something I didn't have.

I pulled out the chair and sat down. The plates were served.

"If Dad were here, he'd be cursing you out for not letting him prepare his own plate," the girl next to me said to Zachary, who was at the other end of the table.

"That's why we adapt our customs when the father-in-law is here."

"They could adapt when I'm here too; I love getting my hands dirty," she said with a playful tone in her voice, and hell, I was starting to differentiate Hazel's tones of voice.

"I don't doubt that." My cousin rolled his eyes; the two had a relationship like that of siblings.

I remained silent, watching the small hands next to me. Hazel pretended not to be there, talking to anyone but me, which was a great relief because when we did talk, it was usually to exchange barbs.

Sitting next to her felt like having all eyes on us since I was next to the woman who was the center of attention.

Savannah and Hazel could be sisters, similar in appearance, but while Savannah was quiet and shy, Hazel was like a little whirlwind, easily conversing and always smiling at everyone.

CHAPTER FIVE

Hazel

Having the president sitting next to me was like having a block of ice there. Although the desire that lingered inside me was to freeze in that ice.

Christopher only spoke when addressed directly.

"Godmother, will you sleep with me tonight?" I turned my face to Sadie, who had hopeful eyes directed at me.

"But godmother didn't bring any clothes." I frowned.

"It's okay, my clothes will fit you." Sadie wanted to wink, but what came out was a blink from both eyes.

"I thought you were going to offer a dress from your mom, although I bet you'd look gorgeous in a princess dress." Obviously, her clothes wouldn't fit me.

"Too true," Sadie confirmed seriously, causing others to burst into laughter.

"Honey, godmother is in the middle of exams; she needs to study," Savannah tried to comfort her daughter.

"How boring." Sadie pouted.

"But godmother promises that as soon as she has some free time, she'll come here for a pajama party, and we can invite Mommy, Grandma, Aunt Natalie..."

"I think they're already..."

"Don't listen." I raised my finger, stopping what Zachary was about to say. "Your dad doesn't know how much fun our pajama parties are."

I winked conspiratorially at Sadie.

"It's because he's a man, godmother," Sadie dismissed her father. "We dance, eat lots of sweets, do hairstyles, makeup..."

"And when do you sleep?" Mr. Arnold, Zachary's father, asked.

"Sleeping is the least of it," I said.

"It's fun; come on, Natalie, mother-in-law, so I don't feel like an old woman next to Sadie's and Hazel's energy."

"No bedtime?" Zachary's mother made a face.

"You can't sleep, Grandma," Sadie was the most excited.

"We can play a lot of *Cyndi Lauper, Roxette.*" I looked at the ladies, knowing they were their favorite singers.

"She knows how to win me over." Natalie smiled.

"There's even room for *Bryan Adams,*" I teased. "I'd marry that man just to hear him sing in my ear every day."

"Me too," Sadie replied, not knowing that would drive her father crazy.

"No, you're not even old enough to think about that."

Soon the subject changed, and our girls' night was set for the following weekend.

The main course was cleared once everyone had finished eating, followed by dessert, which was a kind of chocolate sweet with a bar on top.

My eyes sparkled. Like a good little ant, I took a spoonful and brought it to my mouth, letting a soft sigh escape. I soon took another, believing I was doing it with every spoonful of dessert.

"Do you always do that?" I had to turn my neck to make sure that question was indeed for me.

"Do what?" I asked, confused.

"Those sighs; it's just dessert." He raised an eyebrow subtly.

Christopher's movements were always slow, or so subtle that they were barely noticeable most of the time.

"It's a dessert, that's the thing; it's sweet, I love sweet things." I looked at his plate, which hadn't even been touched, not even a spoonful. "Are you going to tell me you don't like sweets?"

"I'm not into vices; it's just a sweet." He shrugged.

"Well, I have many vices, and that's one of them; I love sweets." I let out a smile, and the president's eyes fell on my mouth.

"I noticed that," Christopher replied, not taking his eyes off my lips.

It was as if he were trapped in his internal dilemmas, a mask that didn't let his true feelings show.

But soon he realized that he had possibly been staring at me for too long and turned his attention back to the dessert that I was sure he wouldn't eat.

I finished mine in seconds; I could be considered a little kid when it came to sweets.

Soon after dinner, I had to say goodbye to everyone because I needed to go back home. I had to spend my Sunday studying and needed a good night's sleep.

I reached into the back pocket of my jeans skirt and took out the key to my truck. The poor thing felt out of place next to those luxurious cars.

Footsteps behind me made me turn my face and see the president, while his men quickly took their places, one of them opening the back door.

I put the key in the lock and opened the truck door.

The tall man passed by me, and his scent overwhelmed my senses. *What a waste of a man...*

I watched him from behind; the suit didn't fit tightly on his body, which was probably due to his well-defined thighs and ample backside. I could bet that man was built like a tank, if he weren't such a primitive who didn't let anyone get close.

"Lost something, Miss Bellingham?" His deep voice pulled me out of my analysis.

Christopher hadn't even seen me staring at him, but as if he had eyes on his back, he noticed my gaze. He turned, and our eyes met.

"I lost my ability to reason, it's true? 12 years of celibacy?" I asked with a hint of mockery.

It wasn't the first time I asked that kind of question, and since he never gave me an answer, everything pointed to one thing: it was true.

"It seems that ability was lost a long time ago, along with common sense," he retorted, making a face.

"You're always so serious; it must be a lack of women in your life..."

"You're always smiling, so should I presume that your bed is adequately filled?"

"Not always, I'd say more like regularly. You know, it's good for the endorphins, boosts your mood. You should try it, Mr. President; after all, it can't be easy running this country." Holding the handle of my truck, I opened the door.

"I don't need that to handle my duties," he responded quickly.

"Well, if you say so, who am I to contradict? I'm sure she wouldn't want you to freeze in time." Without waiting for his response, I jumped into my truck.

I knew I had touched on a forbidden topic. In every interview Christopher gave, he always emphasized that he didn't like to talk about his late wife, as it brought back old memories.

Through the rearview mirror of my truck, I saw him watching me for long seconds before he turned and got into his car.

CHAPTER SIX

Hazel

My week was so hectic that I hardly remembered all the events. The exams were wearing me out; finally, Friday had arrived, my usually wonderful mood was terrible, and I still had another exam that day. Exams should be banned on Fridays.

"Dear, would you come to my house with me to pick up some documents to be digitized? It can be done over the weekend; I know you have exams, but I need this urgently!" Natalie appeared, asking as she leaned against my desk.

"Yes, of course, I can do that." I gave a brief smile.

Digitizing documents wasn't that difficult.

"Can we go now?"

"Yes, can I come with you? *Because* to add to my chaotic week, my truck decided not to start this morning. I need to find a mechanic nearby." I sighed, grabbing my bag from under the desk.

"Of course, if you want, I can even lend you one of our cars until yours is ready." The lady went back into her office to grab her bag.

"*Oh*, you don't have to. That would be pushing it too far."

I was sure that along the way, Natalie would insist a bit more for me to accept, even though she was practically my sister's aunt, she was still just my boss. Although she was a good boss and an amazing person, I didn't want to confuse things.

We got into her car, which had a driver waiting. Those people didn't seem to like driving, or they were always too busy to drive.

Natalie was great company; we spent most of the trip talking, or as my sister would say, *it's hard for anyone not to have a topic with me around because I'm always starting conversations.*

The number of cars parked in front of her house said it all. Christopher was there; he was the one who always had that exorbitant amount of security.

"*Oh*, I forgot that Christopher would be here for dinner; he must have arrived early," Natalie responded to my thoughts.

It was good to know I'd get a glimpse of the delicious Mr. President. I knew I was privileged to have that, after all, who else could be so close to one of the most powerful men? Not to mention his family.

We got out of the car, walking side by side, and the lady opened the door to her house.

"Wait for me in the living room, dear; I'll go to my room to get the documents." I just nodded, knowing where the living room was since I had been there a few times.

My heels echoed on the floor when I entered the living room, seeing the man who was staring into space, while his hand was tracing the ring around his neck.

Christopher was so absorbed in his own world that he didn't even notice I was entering. I stamped my foot a bit harder on the floor, making him look at me. Realizing he wasn't alone, the president quickly tucked the object back inside his shirt.

"I've seen that," I said, not caring about his embarrassment.

"There's nothing I'm hiding," he retorted with an indifferent tone.

"How does it work? Is it like fiddling with that ring and it brings her back to your mind?" There was no mockery in my voice, just genuine curiosity.

"It's none of your business," he said seriously, a bit arrogantly.

"Sorry, I crossed the line," I whispered, his intense blue eyes analyzing me.

"It's better if you stay out of my business, nosy woman. I never asked for your opinion on my life. What do you think you are? Some sort of savior? Don't ever meddle in anything concerning me and my life again. Just because my mother likes you doesn't mean I do. Everything about you irritates me." I widened my eyes, instinctively taking a step back.

Okay, okay, maybe I crossed some boundaries. But did it really need all that gratuitous rudeness? What a jerk.

I think it was the first time I was treated with such arrogance.

"I... I..." I blinked several times, embarrassed. It had been a long time since I felt like that.

I always treated everyone around me well to receive the same in return. My manner might annoy some people, but never to that extent.

"Why don't you just get out of here?" he returned to his arrogance, which made me regain my composure.

"Because, Mr. Perfect, not everything revolves around you. I'm waiting for some documents that your mother is going to give me, and also, stick all that arrogance right up your..."

"Dear?" before I could finish my rant, Mrs. Natalie appeared.

I turned, widening my eyes again.

"*Oh*, I'm sorry Natalie." I felt my cheeks warm. It was hard to get me worked up, but it seemed Christopher had a power like no one else to do just that.

"Did something happen?" the lady wanted to know.

"Nothing, just your assistant being nosy as always," Christopher answered.

"I'd rather be nosy than a big arrogant jerk," I muttered, walking towards the lady, knowing he heard me.

"You'd better watch your tongue. Remember, you still work for my family," the man remained defensive.

"Dear, Hazel is my assistant, and she's wonderful at what she does. I just hope you two can get along at some point because I don't understand the reason for all this conflict," Natalie handed me the papers.

"The reason is clear. She keeps sticking her nose where it doesn't belong. Can't she take care of her own life?" I turned my eyes to him.

"It's fine, Mr. President," I responded curtly. "I deeply hope you drown in your own bitterness."

"As long as you're not around, it will be my pleasure." Christopher turned away.

He left me talking to myself; my body was tense, everything about me was on fire. It was incredible how easily he could pull me out of all my comfort zones.

Slowly, I turned my gaze back to Natalie, feeling guilty at that moment for speaking to her son like that, not because of him, but because of her.

"I'm so sorry." I gave a forced smile.

"It's alright, dear. Christopher is used to everyone agreeing with him, bowing down as if he's the only one with an opinion. I know he treats you this way because you don't fear him. I know my son, Chris is on the defensive. If one day, on any occasion, he ever does anything to you, please let me know." The lady took my hand and escorted me to the door.

It was good to have people in that state to rely on, after all, my parents were far away.

CHAPTER SEVEN

Christopher

If I hadn't made it crystal clear to my family that I wouldn't have the chance to be with another woman, I would swear that Mom was doing it on purpose, bringing Hazel into the same environment I was in.

This fact must have thrown me off a bit because I crossed the line and did something I shouldn't have. I was rude to the woman. I had never acted that way with a woman before, but everything about Hazel drove me crazy; she had the power to piss me off.

Hell!

To avoid leaving any hint that I was moved by the situation, I ended up having dinner with my parents, but my thoughts were constantly focused on my mother's assistant. I believed it was the first time I had thought about another woman for an extended period of time, other than Anna.

"SYDNEY, THIS IS MADNESS," I sighed loudly, running my hand through my hair.

"Christopher, we'll be boarding in Seattle. There's the charity event, and right after, we can head to Chicago. Time is tight, but I know it will work out." My assistant often made tight schedules, which frequently caused a tremendous headache.

"Great, and after Chicago, we'll return to Washington DC since I have a meeting with the senators to discuss the new set of laws to be implemented." I opened the small window of the jet.

"You know that if you're not present, Zachary can take over. — Yes, I knew that, but my cousin wasn't up-to-date on all matters; he might not know my opinions and objections, as we hadn't discussed that issue.

"Why doesn't Zach go to these events? I like the bureaucratic stuff." My voice had a tone of mockery.

"Unless Zachary has your face, he can't do this part because it's your face that the voters want to see, especially if you want to run for re-election in three years." I nodded, knowing it was what I wanted, and it wasn't a secret to anyone.

"I only leave the presidency to hand over the position to another member of my family." A smug smile played on my lips, as when it came to my dedication to politics, I was as proud as could be.

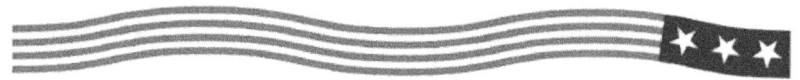

THE WEEKEND WAS SO busy that I didn't even realize it had passed. Slowly, I sat on the huge bed, to which, after twelve years, I had adapted to sleep alone, without the company of any other woman.

Anna hadn't been my only woman in bed; before her, I had been with others. It was just sex, but after her, there was no more room for anyone else in my sheets.

I ran my hand over my neck, feeling the wedding band, not allowing it to be buried with that small symbol of our love.

I always had it with me, but it seemed like in the past few weeks, it had been fading. Her brown eyes didn't appear because, in my mind, they were often replaced by those feline blue eyes. It confused me, drove me crazy.

That was why I had been touching that ring more frequently. I couldn't let Anna die in my thoughts; it was the only place she still lived.

I walked to my closet and put on one of my gym clothes because I needed to channel all that bitterness into something.

Before leaving the room, I went to the suite and washed my face, doing everything I needed there, but I didn't even grab my phone. After all, everyone who worked with me knew I only picked up the device after returning from the gym because if it was something of extreme urgency, they came to me personally.

Walking through the White House corridors, I could have a *personal trainer*, someone by my side 24 hours a day, even while I slept, but it wasn't necessary inside there. That house was safer than any other place, so why did I need more people on my tail? Whenever I could and managed, I liked to be alone.

I pushed open the double doors, finding my gym. I went straight to the treadmill, starting with my run. I turned it on and ran as fast as I could.

My eyes lifted when I saw my cousin coming in.

"Where else would I find you but here? This must be like having sex in your version," Zachary said, mocking as he entered the room.

"Don't you think it's too early to come bother me?" I asked, lowering the treadmill speed.

"Actually, I needed to escape a bit. Too many women at my place for an entire weekend, and it's not the type you're thinking of." Zachary sat on one of the equipment benches.

"Sleepover?" I grimaced, recalling the plans the women had made at that dinner, immediately coming to mind, the feline eyes of the daring woman.

"That's a manual on how to drive a man crazy. I need to have a son so I'm not always surrounded by women."

"Does that mean you're going to try for another child?" I grabbed the towel from the treadmill.

"Of course, we'll only stop when my boy is born. Not that I don't love my daughters, but I need a partner in crime." Zachary laughed loudly.

"And what does Savannah say about that?" I asked, raising an eyebrow.

"Sav wants another child just as much as I do. When I say my wife is too good for me, I'm not being ironic." He burst into another loud laugh.

"You're a lucky bastard." I rolled my eyes.

It wasn't the first time I'd said that, and Zachary was already used to it. We had a camaraderie as if we were brothers.

"I won't say anything. You're too stubborn to understand. By the way, my sister-in-law wants your head. What did you say to her?" Zachary looked at me seriously at that moment.

"I was a bit arrogant with her, and Hazel has every right to be upset, but at least this way, she'll stop messing with my head."

I shrugged my shoulders, trying to show how little I cared, when deep down, I knew I did. The resentful eyes, the way she widened them, taking a step back, not knowing what to say, her expression, it all got to me, and all I could think about was that I had hurt her, and I couldn't understand why it mattered to me so much.

CHAPTER EIGHT

Hazel

"Finally, the exam period is over." I sighed, sitting at the bar table.
"That's why we need to celebrate." My classmate sat down next to me.

"It's not like it won't come around again, but we definitely need a good celebration." I laughed, grabbing that beer mug.

The results of our exams had already been released, and my grades were all above average. That was something to celebrate, after all the sleepless nights living on caffeine. Who said studying law was easy? *Well, I don't think anyone ever said that.*

MY HEAD WAS THROBBING, and the annoying sound of my phone ringing only added to the pain.

I fumbled beside the furniture, grabbing the phone while opening just one eye and seeing my sister's name.

I answered the call grumbling as I put the phone to my ear.

"*Wow, Hazel, how long does it take to answer your phone?*" Savannah immediately began to complain.

"I'm single, and I have the right to a drunken night," I grumbled with my eyes closed.

"*Seriously? Hazel!*" Savannah scolded me.

"Relax, little sis, not everyone is a puritan like you, and I know how to behave. I got drunk and caught a ride home," I whispered, bringing my hand vaguely to my head.

"*Hazel, watch your language.*" Savannah, being the older sister, always took the more authoritative stance.

"You didn't call me on a Saturday morning to lecture me, did you?" I retorted, waiting for her to hang up so I could go back to sleep.

"*No, not at all. Zachary decided to go to the beach, take Sadie for a run on the sand, and enjoy the warmth in Hampton at this time of year. Do you want to come along?*"

"Damn it, Sav, if you had told me that yesterday, I wouldn't have drunk so much," I grumbled, regretting drinking to the last drop as if there were no tomorrow.

"*Take a painkiller, and it'll pass soon. Come on, little sis?*" I could swear she was clasping her hands at that moment.

"*Alright, alright*"— I played a bit of drama. "I can make this sacrifice for you."

I opened my eyes and sat up in bed. I looked around and, with a sigh, got out of bed.

"*Hazel, there's a driver waiting for you. If you can, come quickly.*" Savannah had that tone of voice where she always seemed guilty.

"What do you mean? I didn't agree to anything."

"*We know you love the beach.*" My sister chuckled.

"You know me so well. I'll get dressed, pack my bag quickly, and I'm on my way. But first, I'll take a painkiller. My head is going to explode," I grumbled, heading downstairs where my medications were.

We ended the call, and I hoped I'd remember that pain the next time I decided to drink.

IT WASN'T THE FIRST time we had come to the White House to use their helipad, so I wasn't surprised that we were taking this route; at the very least, the president must be lost in one of those countless rooms.

I had never been inside the enormous house; everything seen from the outside was exactly as in the photos, grand, with huge columns, elegant, a real postcard. It must be wonderful to live in that place.

We drove along the gravel path and arrived at the back of the mansion, where some cars were parked. I swore I didn't know how my sister had gotten used to all that grandeur. It was so far removed from the reality we knew. We were girls from Arizona; although we were dreamers, none of that had ever crossed our minds.

It was clear how much Zachary loved Savannah and that he didn't even care that we came from a social class so much lower than his. Apparently, no one in the Fitzgerald family minded. One of the clear reasons they were one of the most beloved families in the country.

My door was opened when the car stopped, and, using my sunglasses, I got out. At least with them on, my eyes weren't as irritated by the daylight.

"Let me grab your suitcase and take it to the jet, Miss," the driver said as he saw me reaching for my suitcase.

"*Oh...* that's alright," I cleared my throat.

"They're waiting for you inside the jet, Miss," another man approached and said.

I simply nodded and headed for the extended stairs. The wind was mild, and I opted for wearing jeans and white sneakers. My tank top was simple, a comfortable travel outfit, even though I figured it would only be about a 45-minute flight. It was typical of Zachary to do such things, traveling for just a weekend whenever there was a free slot in his schedule.

I climbed one step at a time, with my handbag under my arm.

The voices were audible from inside, and as soon as I entered, I saw a huge jet with double and individual seats, as well as some tables in front of the seats, clearly designed to provide every comfort it could offer.

The presence of Grace and Natalie was not surprising; the ladies loved to travel, bringing their husbands along.

But the presence that surprised me the most was his; the president was there too. *Didn't he have those bureaucratic things to deal with?*

I tried to ignore his presence and focused my attention on my little goddaughter. Sadie was in a seat with her seatbelt fastened.

"Auntie, I saved a seat for you," Sadie clapped her little hands excitedly.

I wasn't sure if I was up for being good company, because even after taking the painkiller, my head was still throbbing.

"Sweetheart, Auntie has a bit of a headache," Savannah spoke to her daughter.

"I'm fine, it's a great excuse to remind me never to drink so much beer again," I grumbled as I sat down next to Sadie.

She was in a double seat, and I sat beside her, placing my bag under the seat.

"The only person who was missing has arrived; now we can go," Zachary said a bit louder, sounding even impatient.

"You're lucky my head hurts too much to question anything," I whispered, taking off my sunglasses and fastening my seatbelt for takeoff.

I knew that soon the pain would pass, but until it did, it felt like I had a monkey banging cymbals in my head.

CHAPTER NINE

Hazel

Sadie talked to me throughout the entire trip, and even if I had wanted to, I wouldn't have been able to sleep; my goddaughter could come up with topics of conversation from a year ago.

At times, I would glance sideways, discreetly, so as not to be noticed, and see the man who was sleeping serenely, or pretending to be asleep.

Christopher wasn't wearing his usual suit. He was dressed in beige khaki pants, paired with a white polo shirt, and the light colors suited him.

Fortunately, I wasn't caught in the act at any moment.

The pilot's announcement echoed over the speaker, instructing us to fasten our seatbelts again as we were about to land.

My goddaughter let out an excited squeal.

I didn't say anything; after all, I was afraid of takeoffs and landings. I held Sadie's little hand with one hand, while the other gripped the armrest a little tighter.

After long seconds, without any fuss, the jet landed. Even though it was nothing, a silly fear or not, it was my fear.

The doors were opened.

I had been to their beach house before. The Fitzgeralds had a vacant lot next to their mansion just for the helipad.

Sadie didn't want me to unfasten her seatbelt, so I waited for her. She was at the stage where she wanted to be independent.

"I did it," she said excitedly, and I almost thanked her.

We got up together, without me worrying about whether there was someone behind me. My back bumped into something, and at the first move, I tripped over my own feet. The large hands that held my waist made me widen my eyes.

The fingers circled my skin firmly, but I quickly composed myself, regaining my movements. I looked up to see that pair of blue eyes glaring at me. He didn't say anything; it was as if he were in another world.

I noticed when he opened and closed his hands, as if repulsed by the act. I took a step to the side, thereby freeing his movement.

"Sorry, I didn't see you," was all that came out of my mouth as Christopher said nothing, walking past me and leaving his perfume lingering in the air.

I turned my face to Sadie; the little one was shrugging her shoulders in confusion.

"Mommy says Uncle Chris is weird," she whispered as if he couldn't hear, but it was just the two of us in there, with no chance of being overheard.

"I think she's right," I teased, giving her a wink.

We got off the jet, the sea breeze touching my body. I loved that house; it was simply perfect, without a single flaw.

Sadie, in her excitement, ran ahead to catch up with her parents, and I lowered my sunglasses. It was mid-morning, and Savannah had woken me up early for the trip, so we would have plenty of time to enjoy.

The men from the jet were handling the luggage while I, along with the others, entered the enormous mansion, where the back faced the sea.

"Can I stay in the same room I stayed in last time?" I asked, knowing it was the guest room. Every family member had their own room there; it was a place used by all the Fitzgeralds.

"Yes, you can, sister, it's just you as a guest today, the others each have their own rooms." I thanked her with a smile. "I'll ask them to take your suitcase there, is that alright?"

"Yes." I nodded my head.

"Auntie, can we go swimming in the pool?" Sadie asked with a hopeful smile.

"Yes, my love, but first, you need to ask your parents since the sun is strong right now." Sadie immediately turned to her parents, who grimaced because the sun was too strong at that moment. "Let's do this: Auntie will enjoy a little sun now, and then in the afternoon, we can play a lot in the pool, what do you think?"

"Yes!" The little one jumped with joy.

"I think I'm kind of useless right now; can I sunbathe?" I asked, looking at the women.

"Just don't forget sunscreen and face protector," Natalie ordered as if she were my mother.

"Yes, boss." I gave a sideways smile. "I can take the opportunity to nap a bit since I was practically kicked out of bed this morning."

I headed to the stairs, knowing where my room was, so there was no need for anyone to accompany me. I walked down the corridor and entered the room where my suitcase was already waiting; I still marveled at how quickly the staff worked.

I stopped in front of my suitcase, opened it, took out my swimsuit, and entered the suite, slowly removing my clothes. I touched my waist where the president's large hands had been; it had to be madness—how could I be so affected by a man like that? And the worst part was, he constantly snubbed me, not to mention the time he practically ignored me at his parents' house.

I would be strong and pretend to be uninterested in the fact that he had touched me.

I tied my hair into a bun and turned in front of the mirror. The swimsuit was perfect, accentuating my medium breasts, but not vulgar;

after all, I was in a family home. The bottom part covered my butt appropriately. I went back to the room and grabbed a beach cover-up, which was a loose dress.

I put my sunglasses back on and grabbed the sunscreen and bronzer. I would use them when I was on the lounger. I put on my flip-flops, holding my phone in one hand and the tubes of sunscreen in the other, and left the room.

My intention was to head straight to the pool, to the corner where almost no one passed, so I could lie on my stomach and at least catch a little sleep.

I arrived at the loungers, with the sun blazing down. I sat on one and took off my cover-up. The bronzer was spray-on, just like the sunscreen, which made it easy to apply.

Slowly, I applied it all over my body while looking up as a shadow fell across me.

I didn't take off my sunglasses, but I was tempted to, just to get a glimpse of the tall man in front of me.

"We need to talk," he said immediately.

"At this moment? No!" I retorted.

"Yes, at this moment."

"You're blocking my sun, if you don't mind." Ignoring his presence completely, I lay down on the lounger.

Perfect, by doing that, Christopher would think I didn't even care about his distinguished presence.

CHAPTER TEN

Christopher

I shouldn't have gone to talk to that woman; it was clear she was angry with me. I wanted at least to do what anyone would do in my situation: apologize for the way I treated her. It was a matter of good manners.

Turn around and leave! My conscience screamed at me, but instead of doing that, I lowered my gaze, focusing on her small body, on the way the swimsuit hugged her curves. Her head was turned away from me, her hair tied up in a bun, her back smooth, her skin looking silky. For the first time since losing my wife, my fingers itched, an itch that would only be satisfied if I touched those curves.

But I couldn't!

I couldn't touch Hazel; she embodied everything I hated in a woman, not physically, but temperamentally—her liveliness, her flamboyance, always being the center of attention, not to mention her sharp tongue, as if she always wanted to be the main attraction. Hazel Bellingham was and would never be for me! And that was obvious.

Without looking at the point I was sure would be my surrender, which could shake all my stability, I turned my back, avoiding lustfully looking at her ass.

Damn it! Zachary didn't say she would be here; if I had known, I wouldn't have come. It was supposed to be a weekend of rest, not torture.

I walked toward the house bar; a strong dose of whiskey would do me good.

I quickly grabbed my favorite bottle, filled half a glass, and set my phone aside, drinking the whole thing in one go.

I noticed movement beside me; it was my father.

"Pour me a drink," he said, sitting on a stool. The bar was outside the house, as if it were a small place reserved just for men.

I did as he asked, placing the glass in front of him, pulling up a stool, and sitting across from my father with the whiskey bottle beside me.

"Are you having another drink?" he asked, seeing me refill my glass.

"Two drinks won't get me drunk," I whispered.

"The issue is that it's still morning, and you're having two drinks." Our eyes met.

"I have a good eating routine; it won't hurt me," I declared, bringing the glass to my mouth.

"What's going on, son? We've always been good friends; you know you can tell me anything you don't want to share with your mother," Dad said in that familiar tone of voice, the same one he used since I was a child.

"It's nothing, Dad," I mumbled.

"We know it's something." He looked beyond the glass windows; I did the same, seeing him look at the woman lying there. "Why is it that every time Hazel is around, you end up on the defensive?"

"I don't like the way she thinks so highly of herself." I shrugged my shoulders.

"That shouldn't bother you; after all, nothing affects you, but that woman, yes, she bothers you." We looked at each other again.

"Yes, and that's all, there's no other reason," I tried to brush off the topic.

"Christopher..." Dad sighed, knowing I was hiding something, that I wouldn't delve into the topic.

If I didn't talk about Hazel, nothing would become real. Anna was real; she was the love of my life. I was sure this would all pass soon; that girl must just be acting that way because she was bold, like something I never had before.

"Alright, I know you'll want to talk about it at the right moment, and know that I'll be here to listen." He got up from his stool, drank all the whiskey, and turned, leaving me alone with my dilemmas.

The thought of lying that something unexpected came up flashed in my mind, so I could escape like a good coward from the woman under that sun. As if she needed that, if she were mine, I'd never let her sunbathe! *Damn it! Hazel was and would never be mine.*

I left my empty glass on the counter, went back into the house, staying as far away from the woman as possible.

The smell of food was in the air. I turned my face towards the kitchen, which was connected to the dining room and living room, watching the cooks working there. Our beach house was well-ventilated, with many glass doors letting in the sea breeze.

Sadie was in the middle of the room playing with her toys, the baby in her mother's arms, while the women chatted animatedly, and my presence was barely noticed.

Holding my phone, I looked up the number for the pier's central office where our boats were kept. Going out and spending the day away would be better than returning to Washington DC, and that way no one would be suspicious.

"Got something on your mind?" Zachary approached me.

"I'm thinking of taking a boat ride," I said honestly, assuming he wouldn't be coming.

"You could take Hazel with you, couldn't you?"

"Of course not!" I believed I was too quick in my response, which made my cousin frown.

"What's the problem? The boat is huge; everyone will be in their own corner. I bet you won't even bump into each other. Hazel wanted to take a boat ride last time we were here, and since Savannah doesn't like those things, she can't join us," my cousin tried to find a pretext.

"The answer remains no, I don't want her beside me." I let out a long, deep sigh, trying to distance myself from him.

Quickly, I moved away from Zachary because the last thing I needed was wanting some peace and taking the source of all my frustration with me. That would be madness.

I didn't know what was going through my family's minds, but I was becoming more and more certain that they were pushing me into the arms of that crazy woman.

Given that realization, it was better if I didn't apologize, as doing so might open the door for her to start provoking me again.

CHAPTER ELEVEN

Hazel

I spent the afternoon with Sadie by the pool. My goddaughter had practically everyone playing ball with her during her bath. Except for the president, who was important enough to stay away from mere mortals like us and went out for a boat ride.

Zachary said he told Christopher to invite me along, since the last time we were at the beach house, I was enchanted by the boats at the pier as we passed by. But obviously, Mr. Perfect would never accept my company.

I kept wondering how he could come from such a close-knit family when all he did was shut himself off in his own little world.

I put on a sandal as I left the room, leaving my hair loose and damp, not bothering to dry it. The dress I chose hung loosely on my body. The night outside was mild, with a pleasant sea breeze.

I went down the stairs, my eyes observing the outside through the open curtains. I could see the men by the pool chatting, and there was the untouchable president.

"You look beautiful, dear." I smiled at Natalie, who was waiting for me at the bottom of the first step.

"Thank you." I returned the smile.

"Can I ask you something?" Natalie glanced around to make sure no one was listening.

"Yes, go ahead." I furrowed my brows in confusion.

"Is something going on between you and my son?"

"I don't understand, what do you mean by that?" I asked, still not getting it.

"I mean, it seemed like he ran away from here today." She continued to look discreetly around.

"*Oh*, nothing happened. After that day when he was a real jerk, we haven't spoken again; in fact, I'd rather keep my distance from him." I shrugged my shoulders.

It was already hard enough seeing his image on every site, magazine, and media outlet. Now, seeing the man who clearly told me to my face that I was unbearable and didn't like me was humiliating.

"Are you sure that's all?" Mrs. Natalie wanted to find out if there was more behind it all.

"Yes, there's nothing to hide." I gave my best convincing smile, even though I wanted to curse Christopher, to talk about how he thought he owned the world. The worst part was that he practically did while being president.

"Then I'm relieved." She invited me to have a glass of champagne, but all I wanted for the night was to avoid anything with alcohol, so I ended up declining.

I left the house and approached one of the hammocks, pulled the fabric, and sat down with my phone in hand. I fiddled with it while no one missed me until my sister showed up.

"Hazel, will you watch Alexis while I feed Sadie?" Savannah could have a nanny for absolutely everything, but she still insisted on doing the essential tasks in her daughters' lives.

I got up and took the little girl in my arms.

"Come with Auntie, my angel." I smiled at the little girl who was discovering her fingers by putting them in her mouth. "You can go, sister, I'll call you only if she gets hungry."

Savannah thanked me and went inside. With Alexis in my arms, I started walking across the lawn toward the edge of the sand, where the grass ended and the beach began.

"It's so nice to be a baby," I whispered affectionately to my niece.

I was only Alexis's godmother. Scarllet, Zachary's sister, was Alexis's godmother. But I loved them both equally. Since Alexis was still a baby, my stronger connection was with Sadie.

"Can we talk now?" That voice I knew so well echoed behind me.

"We have nothing to talk about," I whispered without turning around.

"I need to apologize for being rude that day." It seemed like he didn't understand the meaning of not wanting to talk.

"You don't need to apologize," I said while still looking at the sea.

"Yes, I do. I've never treated anyone like that." I wasn't going to turn my face, not going to look at that man, who, besides being handsome, smelled wonderful.

"You did your part, Mr. President, now you can go back." I murmured, keeping my gaze fixed on Alexis, who was still with her fingers in her mouth.

"No, this isn't a duty. I just want you to forgive me for acting wrong with you." He seemed to deepen his voice, a recurring habit when he lost his patience.

"Since you're not going to leave, I will." I turned, ignoring the man for the second time that day.

"Hazel." I think that was the first time I heard him call me by my first name, as if it were a plea, a request for a truce.

I turned and raised my eyes to meet his. Christopher had all the world's charm with the moonlight reflecting on his face, his dark hair slightly tousled, his blue eyes staring at me.

"You asked me to stop being intrusive; that's what I'm doing, Mr. Fitzgerald. Don't come playing the remorseful man, the type who chases after someone when they're snubbed. We know that's not your style. Even if you say it was all a lie, I don't believe it. We've always exchanged barbs; you don't need to come now to apologize for something we both knew. We can't stand each other; you're irritatingly perfectionistic, and I think I'm always right, so we don't need to get along, nor to talk. Just do what you do best, keep ignoring me," I stopped speaking, gasping for breath.

Fortunately, he didn't argue. Maybe he realized that everything I said was true. He might be the most handsome, the most perfect physically, but inside, he was a man completely shut off from everything, and it wouldn't be me who would touch that armored heart, if anyone ever could.

My niece settled into my lap, and to my surprise, Alexis fell asleep without me even noticing.

I went back inside the house, smelling the delicious aroma of dinner.

CHAPTER TWELVE

Hazel

I closed the door to Sadie's room carefully. She fell asleep quickly, and I had asked Savannah if I could put the little one to bed so she could just focus on Alexis.

The hallway light illuminated the entire area, and I looked up as I saw the door to one of the rooms open. It had to be a joke; it seemed that being in the same house wasn't enough; we had to keep bumping into each other.

I quickly turned my back on him and headed in the opposite direction, making my way to my room, which was in another hallway in the guest area.

Fortunately, Christopher took my sudden turn as a "I'll leave you alone" gesture.

Or maybe not, since I liked to poke at him, but I had promised myself I wouldn't do that anymore.

I entered the room, breathless. I went to the bathroom, washed my face, brushed my teeth, and opened my suitcase again, pulling out one of my pajamas. Most of my sleepwear was modest, a pair of shorts with a top.

I didn't have a sensual type; all the cases I had were just sex, except for Luck. He was my first school boyfriend; we were together from when I was 15 until I was 17. I couldn't even say it was love. Luck was my first man in bed, and he was so clumsy that I didn't get any pleasure at all; in fact, with Luck, there was never any pleasure. I was too young, thought sex was something obligatory. My mother was never one to talk about those things, and my sister lost her virginity to the man who got her pregnant, namely Zachary.

I always knew everything theoretically; I knew how to take care of myself, knew how everything worked.

When I started college, Luck broke up with me because we were going to different schools, which was somewhat of a relief.

After Luck, I had three more men in three years. It wasn't something I felt was obligatory at that stage of life; I learned that I didn't need to have sex out of obligation, without pleasure. So, I only did it when I really wanted to and felt that the man would also give me pleasure.

I turned off the bedroom light, leaving only the bedside lamp on, and lay down on the bed. I tossed and turned for a while and realized I couldn't sleep. Sleeping in that lounge chair had definitely left me wide awake.

The house seemed to be in silence. I got out of bed. I could go to the kitchen and have a glass of milk; Dad always said it helped with sleep.

I walked silently down the hallway, barefoot, but didn't find anyone on the way. When I reached the stairs, I noticed the lights were off; however, the outside light illuminated the inside faintly, but it was enough for me to get to the kitchen without needing to turn anything on.

I easily entered the kitchen, grabbed a glass from the cabinet, and went to the fridge, opening it and taking out the milk jug. I placed the glass on the counter and filled it with the white liquid, while putting the milk back and heading to the island where the stools were, sitting on one to drink my milk.

I sipped a few times, heard some footsteps, and everything was silent. Because of that, I could hear what was going on around me, and when I saw the tall figure of the man, I almost let out a forced laugh. It had to be a joke.

"What are you doing here?" he was the first to ask.

"I came for a glass of milk." I gently lifted the glass, showing it.

"Can't sleep?" Christopher was standing near the island, at the end of it, away from where I was.

"Yeah, I guess sleeping in the morning didn't do me any good." I shrugged my shoulders and took a bigger gulp of my milk, hoping to finish it quickly so I could sleep.

"Or you shouldn't get drunk. Women like you shouldn't subject themselves to that kind of thing. You don't know the danger you're in doing that." His tone seemed somewhat controlling.

"And you, do you?" I couldn't resist and ended up asking.

"Yes, some man could approach you, they might abuse your body without your consent." He was blunt.

"I can take care of myself very well, and what did you mean by women like me?" I jumped off the stool, ready to curse him if he called me vulgar or anything like that.

"Beautiful."

Okay, that caught me off guard, and even though I had promised myself not to make that kind of comment, I ended up losing my composure and said:

"You think I'm beautiful, Mr. President?" I smiled with a mix of mockery.

"Only a blind man wouldn't admit that."

"Right, now you're generalizing," I muttered, losing all hint of malice. After all, he compared me and said it was what all men might think.

I took the glass to my mouth, drank it all in one gulp, and put it in the sink.

"So, how did you know I was here?" I asked, turning my body and noticing he was still in the same spot.

"I was working on the sofa; you walked by and didn't see me sitting."

"I think I would have seen if you were there." I frowned.

"My laptop is over there; you can check for yourself." He pointed, and I leaned over to see.

The house was dim, but the light from the laptop was clear. How did I not see it?

I shook my head. That wasn't my business. Without wanting to cross any of his boundaries, I simply headed toward the stairs. Our relationship had never been good, but after what he said at his mother's house, it had become terrible.

If I used to love provoking him, now I didn't know how to react.

"Hazel," he called my name.

It was like experiencing a new sensation hearing my name coming from his lips.

"You're forgiven, Mr. President, if that's what you want," I grumbled, turning around and being startled to realize he was very close to me, *too close.*

"I need to do something, I need to know that this isn't just in my head." The man abruptly moved his face closer to mine.

My eyes widened, and I took a step back; he hadn't even touched me, he only wanted to kiss me—was that really it? Did Christopher want to kiss me to settle a doubt of his?

"Have you gone crazy? What did you intend to do?" I asked immediately.

"Wasn't it obvious? I was going to kiss you," he said as if it were just a casual kiss.

"First, you disdain me, hate me from the first moment you laid eyes on me, and now, to clear up a doubt, you think you can just kiss me?" I took another step back, ensuring we wouldn't be close again.

"I thought it was what you wanted too," he must have been joking.

"Be your test? Thanks, but I don't want to be a test for any man. It's better if you look for someone else," I grumbled, turning and quickly climbing those stairs, practically running toward my room.

My heart was racing. Had I just rejected the President of the United States' kiss? All because I didn't want to be a test for him?

I must be crazy, but I didn't regret that craziness; after all, this way we wouldn't have to look at each other and remember that we had shared a kiss.

CHAPTER THIRTEEN

Christopher

What the hell was going on in my head? How could I have considered kissing that woman? And worse, I got my kiss rejected. What did she think? How could she turn me down?

Hell, I should be grateful she refused to kiss me.

I turned my back and grabbed my notebook from the couch. That incident still dazed my mind. I had her so close, even in the dim light, I could see her sparkling blue eyes.

I didn't touch her; I couldn't do that. The kiss was already too much of a novelty; caresses went far beyond what I had planned.

It wasn't a test; in reality, it was what I wanted to do. I would never, in my right mind, kiss a woman without truly wanting to.

I used the word "test" to make her think I was being practical. As if it were an act I didn't really want.

At first, the word *test* was what harmed me, and it was my fault. She wasn't to blame; I was the one who erred.

I shouldn't have approached her like that. For the first time since Anna left me, Hazel was the first woman I wanted to kiss.

The most crazy, most wrong woman was the first one my body chose to kiss.

I wanted to convince myself that it was my body, not my mind, nothing that was so intense and would possibly pass soon.

What I did today was a mistake. Before taking any action with any woman, I needed to end something.

I went up the stairs, grabbed my phone, and requested that my jet be prepared. I needed to go to California, where she was.

I JUST INFORMED MY parents that I was leaving because I needed to deal with my problems, something that was solely mine, my torments.

I used my private jet, as there was no need to use the larger one when it was just me.

I spent the entire journey thinking about what I would do, knowing that one day this moment would come, the time for a final goodbye. I never did it because a part of me wanted to keep her forever, but that part was no longer as strong, the memories weren't as vivid in my mind and seemed to dissipate like mist.

My mistake was thinking that a person like her could appear in my life, someone who completed me like Anna did. But that never happened.

Not even with Hazel did it seem the same; that woman was like a unique entity. Hazel couldn't even be compared to anyone else, just like my Anna, both were unique in their personalities.

Why the hell was I comparing the two? What was the reason for that damn woman not leaving my thoughts?

Anna was the woman of my life, but Hazel was nothing! The confusion was driving me insane.

And if that wasn't enough, there I was, at the place where my Anna used to be, the same place I visited almost once a month or whenever I needed some time alone, a spot to vent.

I stopped in front of her tombstone, with the name *Anna Smith-Fitzgerald* inscribed on it.

I looked around; as I had asked the caretaker, I didn't want anyone present. Since it was my wife there, it was a person of complete trust who took care of the cemetery. And I was never photographed there.

I knelt and placed a bouquet of red roses for her because they were her favorites.

My fingers touched the small tombstone; I no longer cried, there were no tears left to shed. My sadness had taken them all away.

I ran my hand behind my neck and removed the necklace, while the small ring glittered in the palm of my hand where I placed it. That was where Anna's finger used to be, in the middle of the ring.

I felt like I was betraying Anna by wearing that and thinking of someone else. Even though I would never do anything with Hazel, just thinking about her felt like a betrayal.

On the grass, I placed the ring, leaving it next to her tombstone.

"*I will always love you, my Anna. You know I will always love you. I have been faithful to you all these years, but in my heart, I feel it's time to move on. However, I promise with all my heart that I won't be a complete bastard, after all, that's what you used to call me before we met.*" The memory made me smile crookedly.

As a good Fitzgerald, I had my phase of picking up all the women before meeting Anna.

I turned my hand, seeing my wedding ring there, I had never removed it. Maybe if I had removed it at that moment, it could have caused some commotion. But I slowly removed the ring, placing it beside her ring, leaving them there, side by side, as it should have been, but fate didn't want it that way.

The caretaker knew I would leave something there and, by my order, it was not to be removed. As the rains came, the rings would slowly sink, staying forever beside Anna.

She would always be the first woman in my life, but after twelve years since our farewell, it was time for me to move on.

Alone, with the emptiness on my neck, she was no longer with me, but that's how it should be. I took too long; for years, I prolonged that decision. Even if I never had another woman, I knew I would have ended that circle.

There would always be a phase when she was mine, and I was hers. I loved that woman with all my strength, loved our child who remained so small in her belly. Anna's pregnancy was so recent that the sex wasn't even discovered, and I preferred it that way; after all, I would never know if it was a boy or a girl.

Fate was cruel to me, taking away my wife and my child.

I needed to be strong, needed to move on. I knew it was what she would want because she always told me, *never deprive yourself if I'm ever gone; I don't want you to suffer for my absence.*

I kissed my hand and placed it on the tombstone, as if kissing it.

"*I will always cherish the years we spent together, and even if I find someone else, know that I will be grateful for making me the happiest man for all the days we shared.*" I whispered, slowly rising.

I brushed my knees, clearing the bits of grass that had stuck there.

That was the goodbye I should have given a long time ago, but it was necessary to wait for my heart's timing, for the pain to soothe my soul.

I didn't know what to do with my life, nor what tomorrow would bring, but one thing I was sure of was that I couldn't stand the image of that damn woman with the bold mouth in my mind anymore.

CHAPTER FOURTEEN

Hazel

Spending the weekend at the beach was rejuvenating, even though I was hungover on Saturday morning; it didn't interfere with anything.

It wasn't even new to me to wake up on Sunday and not find the President at the house. He was probably lamenting having betrayed his deceased wife; after all, what can you expect from a man who reserved himself for someone who is already gone?

I packed my bag, putting a college book inside because after work I would always come home and then head to college.

I put on one of my suits, wearing tights to cut through the chill. It wasn't very cold in Washington DC, but even the slight chill made me shiver.

Holding my bag under my arm, I left my house. I quickly headed to my truck, huddled up by rubbing my hands together, and checked my phone to see it was nine degrees at that moment.

I started the car; maybe it would have been better if it were newer and the heater worked properly.

I turned on the engine, increased the volume of the car radio, and listened to the news. That was all it could play, but I didn't mind the lack of a USB port.

What caught my attention was the mention of the President:

"*President Christopher Fitzgerald attended Madame Lins's charity event. The man, who was always reserved about his personal life, did not overlook the fact that he was not wearing his wedding ring. Even though his wife had passed away, he had always worn it."*

Okay, that was news. After all, as far as I remembered, he had been wearing the ring on Saturday at the beach house.

What could be the reason for him being without it?

I continued listening to the radio, curious to know if he was accompanied. Usually, Christopher was either with his assistant or never with another woman.

I didn't know who Madame Lins was, but she must have been important for him to have gone without his ring. I wasn't sure why, but a hint of jealousy bubbled up inside me.

Even with the radio on, they didn't mention anything more about the President.

I entered the office parking lot, and my hidden spot was always waiting for me.

I parked my truck, practically ran to the entrance, and my smile widened as I greeted the receptionist.

I loved that office for always being warm on cold days.

I turned on the computer, prepared Mrs. Fitzgerald's coffee, setting everything up, but as soon as I sat in my chair, Natalie arrived with her usual smile on her face.

"Good morning, dear." I handed her the coffee I had left on my desk.

"Good morning, Natalie, your usual coffee." I returned the smile.

"Today is a day of joy." The woman's eyes clearly showed how radiant she was.

"And may I know the reason?" I leaned in, hoping it was something related to the President; I admitted I enjoyed talking about him.

"Chris removed his ring. Although we don't know why yet, since he's been very mysterious lately, but that doesn't matter; he's taking a new step." Natalie took a sip of her drink.

"Oh, could it be that he's finally going to find a First Lady?" I continued with my curiosity.

"At Madame Lins's event, he didn't seem to be with any woman in sight. As always, he was closed off in his own world; I don't know, if he does have a woman, he's hiding her very well, which is not his style. When he started dating Anna, we all knew just by looking at him." The lady lost herself in her thoughts. "Anna was a good woman."

Her smile turned sad; it was clear that everyone liked Christopher's late wife, which made me feel ungrateful for sometimes desiring the President.

As our conversation ended, Natalie went into her office.

Before starting my work, I texted my sister to see if she knew anything since Zachary and Christopher were cousins; maybe they had shared something.

I continued with my work, forgetting about my phone at that moment.

"MAY I HAVE THE HONOR of your company for lunch today?" Ethan asked, leaning over my desk, and I looked up at him. "I know how to be persistent."

"I'm noticing that." I gave a half-smile. "Since I promised I'd have lunch with you, I'll accept the invitation. My exams are over, and I have some free time."

I put the pen away and shut down my computer.

"I'll take you to a new restaurant; only high-profile people go there," he said proudly.

Actually, I didn't pay much attention to that kind of thing. What I really enjoyed was being in a good place with great conversation and company, and having those three things was already perfect.

"I'm curious to check it out, but I'll say right now, I don't mind going to a simpler restaurant." I smiled to the side and stood up from my chair.

I grabbed my bag.

"Only the best for you." He winked.

"Ethan." I sighed, having already told him not to get his hopes up because I didn't get involved with men from my workplace, and I didn't want that to complicate things further, especially since I liked Mrs. Natalie so much.

"Don't worry, I remember very well what you asked me, and I won't cross any boundaries unless you ask," Ethan's insistence was something to be envied.

"Shall we take the same car?" I asked, quickly changing the subject.

"Yes, we'll take mine. No offense to your truck, but mine is a bit more discreet." He gave a side smile.

"Got it." I nodded, as my truck did attract attention wherever it went.

"There's my car." He pointed with his finger.

It was a casual Audi model, an ordinary car for any American.

Ethan even opened the passenger door for me to get in; the upholstery smelled of his cologne. It wasn't anything compared to Christopher's, but it was still distinctly masculine.

Comparing Ethan to the President was, in a way, unfair.

CHAPTER FIFTEEN

Hazel

Ethan parked in front of a luxurious restaurant, and when he said it was that style, I didn't expect it to be quite so elegant.

"Ethan, are you sure you want to come to this place?" I pulled my lip to the side; after all, I wasn't dressed appropriately for such a venue.

"Yes, I am." Ethan got out of the car, walked around, and opened my door.

"I don't want you to be upset. I'm not disliking the place, just unsure if I'm dressed appropriately." Indiscreetly, he let his gaze travel down my body, as if my comment were an invitation for him to assess me.

"You look perfect, Hazel, no flaws." With a wave of his hand, he motioned for me to follow him.

Ethan was a good colleague; I hoped our lunch would be pleasant. We stopped at the reception, and since we arrived a bit early, there was a table available.

I should have heeded Savannah's advice: if I didn't want anything with him, I shouldn't encourage him. But the problem was that I had a hard time saying no for too long; it was as if I felt I owed something.

Pulling out my chair, he played the perfect gentleman. Our table was just for two, so we sat facing each other.

"What's the dish of the day?" Ethan immediately asked the waiter who had stopped beside us.

The man listed all the dishes, leaving the choice up to us. Since there were a few things I didn't recognize, I ended up choosing the same as Ethan, trusting his taste.

Once we were alone again, Ethan wanted to order wine for both of us, but I didn't think it was a good idea since I would be working afterward, so I opted for a juice.

Even though it was just a glass of wine, I didn't want to go to work right after knowing I had consumed alcohol; that wasn't my style.

Unlike me, Ethan decided to have wine.

Before our dishes even arrived, there was a commotion at the door, and curiously but discreetly, I turned my face and noticed the tall figure among the men, clearly recognizing the President. He was with other men in suits.

There was no need for him to stop at the reception because a woman almost ran to them and greeted them with a big smile on her lips.

I didn't blame her; it was impossible not to give a silly smile in front of that man. I also recognized his assistant standing beside him; she was like his shadow, everywhere he went. Did that poor woman even have a life?

Noticing my companion's impatience, I turned my face toward him.

"These Fitzgeralds were born with a silver spoon in their mouth," Ethan grumbled, his voice tinged with a hint of jealousy.

"My sister is a Fitzgerald, if you don't remember," I stated, noticing that he didn't recall, as his cheeks turned red.

I subtly lifted my face as the men passed by us; it seemed they were heading to one of the larger and more elegant tables.

Christopher sat at the head, which was no surprise given that he was the President of the country.

CHAPTER SIXTEEN

Christopher

When I agreed to go to that lunch, I didn't expect to find that girl there. In fact, it was the last place I thought Hazel would be, and worse, she was accompanied.

It wasn't as if we had anything, since all we had was a near-kiss, which I had crossed all boundaries to prove something to myself.

Hell!

I couldn't focus on my lunch with my attention entirely on the table next to us.

"Fitzgerald"—Sydney beside me called out through a cough, making it clear she wasn't paying attention.

I turned my eyes to the men present. They were a few senators who had come to Washington DC for a meeting. Since we had been in meetings all morning, we decided to go out for lunch. My assistant recommended this new restaurant that had recently opened. That was why we came here, but I didn't expect to find my cousin's sister-in-law right there.

I talked for several seconds until our dishes were served.

"Is there a problem I should know about?" Sydney asked quietly beside me so that no one could overhear.

"Why would there be?" I raised my eyebrow slightly.

"Starting with the fact that you took off your wedding ring and didn't tell me anything," she grumbled that part.

Sydney always knew everything about my life, but that wasn't something I wanted to discuss with others, so I kept it to myself. Even as the President, I believed there were small reasons I could keep private.

"There's no specific reason, just decided to take a new path for myself." I shrugged my shoulders.

"Yes, but this new path could affect your reelection." Her eyes narrowed in my direction.

"This is my first year as President; I believe we can leave that problem for another time," my voice came out somewhat harsh.

We could have a friendship beyond the work she did for my image. But not everything was as it seemed. Sydney was good at what she did but tended to think that everything had problems, that nothing could escape her notice.

"I don't like any of this. You know very well that we have all your moves planned; you can't just think it's nothing," she said in the end.

Fortunately, our brief discussion was interrupted by a senator who started a discussion about the implemented laws.

That was a relief; I could pay attention and still keep my eyes on the table next to us. She wasn't too close, which made it easier to just turn my eyes and see her.

Hazel was facing a man. I knew who he was, or rather, I remembered his features; he was one of the office staff, an attorney, though I couldn't recall his name.

It was clear from his gaze that he wanted much more than a dinner with the blonde. That made my blood boil, without even knowing why.

Hazel wasn't mine; we hadn't had anything. How could I feel as if I had some power over her?

I was jealous, that was evident within me. I wasn't new to this; I had been a passionate man, devoted to a woman, and knew that bitter feeling growing inside me.

I was never one for calmness, much less for being an understanding man when it came to jealousy. Even when I was married, I always made it clear how jealous I was and hated when another man approached my wife.

Hazel was wearing one of the typical outfits she always wore at the office. It seemed that since I took off my ring, it was no longer so unfair to look at the woman, obviously keeping my gaze discreet.

It was incredible how she could be so graceful and walk divinely in those heels, her long hair flowing down her back. Both of them stood up from their chairs and headed towards the reception. I internally begged that she would at least look back and see that I was there.

When she finally turned her gaze, I met those intense blue eyes, as if Hazel knew I was watching her.

Focusing my attention on her back, I noticed the exact moment the man placed his hand there. I clenched my fists, damn it!

I hadn't felt that sensation in a long time; I was angry, a feeling of possession overtaking me, something that didn't even belong to me but that I wanted to be mine!

I didn't know what it was, maybe it was simply the fact that she always provoked me, and now that I no longer had her, my mind was reacting in a not-so-good way.

The two left the restaurant, and I didn't even continue eating my food, focusing entirely on their movements.

They got into the same car, which he opened the door for her to get in. *Damn!*

And so they drove away, and without realizing it, I still had my hands clenched into fists under the table as if I could get up from that chair at any moment and punch the man who thought he could make a move on the woman who should be mine!

I fixed my eyes on the men in front of me, realizing that Sydney was keeping her attention on me. It wouldn't be long before she discovered everything that was happening with me.

My assistant was good at what she did, knew me better than anyone, and it was clear that something was happening with me. However, the worst part was that I couldn't control myself; my expressions revealed that I was far from happy about the situation.

My hunger had ceased, and in my mind, I kept replaying the fact that she had rejected that kiss. Was it because she was in a relationship or because of that man? From the time I watched, they didn't seem to be having an affair. Hazel even appeared somewhat uncomfortable, or that's what I perceived, or rather, what I wanted to understand.

My Monday was turning out to be something I hadn't expected, a real chaos. I hated feeling jealous over something that didn't even belong to me.

After lunch, we all returned to the White House, but deep down, I knew what I would end up doing by the end of the day.

CHAPTER SEVENTEEN

Hazel

Throughout my dinner with Ethan, I could feel Christopher's eyes on us. The reason? *I didn't know.*

It was still a mystery why he was without his wedding ring. It even seemed like big news to the journalists who were eager to know if the president had finally found a new woman in his life.

I closed my agenda; Natalie had completed all her appointments for the day. Since it was a busy afternoon, I hadn't had time to review any of the office's legal cases.

I turned off the computer, swiveled in my chair as the door opened, and squinted my eyes at the distinguished presence of the president.

I quickly opened my agenda, though I didn't remember Natalie having any appointments with him.

"President Fitzgerald." I greeted him with a nod.

I wasn't sure how to react after our encounter at the beach house, but I wouldn't let it change anything; I would continue to be the same, as if nothing had happened.

"Miss Bellingham." He looked toward his mother's office door.

"Should I call your mother and ask if she forgot to schedule something with you?" I raised my eyebrow.

Christopher let out a long sigh. Our eyes met, as if he wanted to say something.

"Actually, you don't need to call." He clasped his hands, interlocking them in front of his body.

Christopher was a tall man, and in that suit, he seemed even more imposing, or maybe it was just me being obsessed with the beauty of that man.

"Do you need something?" I asked, standing up from the chair and leaving the agenda on the counter.

I bent down to grab my purse from the floor, but didn't get a response from Christopher, as Ethan entered the room, knocking on the door.

"*Oh*, President Fitzgerald," he said, extending his hand to Christopher, who looked at him, clearly not remembering his name, an act that even Ethan noticed. "I'm Ethan Miller. You must be surrounded by many men; it must be hard to remember names."

"You're right." That was all he said, not even offering a proper greeting.

What did I miss? Why didn't Christopher like Ethan? After all, as far as I knew, he was a good employee and had never caused problems.

"*Oh*... right," Ethan turned his gaze to me. "You left this in my car today."

He handed me my earring, and I touched my ear, realizing I had indeed lost it.

"*Wow*! Thanks, I didn't realize I had lost it." I reached out and took it.

It was probably when I bent down to pick up my phone that had fallen to the floor.

"*Well*, see you tomorrow." Ethan clapped his hands at his sides, stepping back and leaving my office.

I looked up at the president who was still there and put in my earring, noticing that he was observing my movements.

"Mr. Fitzgerald?" I called out again, realizing that the man wasn't even moving.

"Are you seeing Mr. Miller?" he suddenly asked, making me widen my eyes.

"Why would I answer your question? It's none of your business!" The way I spoke made him cross his arms.

"You refused to kiss me, and now I know why..."

"Know? Really know?" I cut him off roughly.

"Yes, I know. Next time, you could tell me that you're with another man."

"Why would I mention it when it's none of anyone's concern!?"

"Yes! I should know, *I should*!" he said, repeating the word in a way that made him seem like he wanted to own everything.

"*Oh, really*? And why should I? You're the President of the country, not the president of people's lives," I challenged him without revealing my true situation.

"You know what? Screw it. If you want to be with that man, then be with him!" he growled, as if he were even snarling.

"Yes, Mr. Fitzgerald, *I will*, I'll be with whoever I want." Who did he think he was to come to my workplace and question who I was seeing? Even though I wasn't actually seeing Ethan, and that office belonged to his family.

Christopher didn't say anything more; he just turned and left, leaving me there alone, not understanding the reason for that confrontation, not knowing why he had come there.

I clutched my purse under my arm and left the office, not even looking around. I could say that the president got what he wanted; he left me extremely irritated. Who did he think he was? He was nothing, absolutely nothing to me!

What did we have? A brief moment when he wanted to steal a kiss from me, with no touches, no anything, a kiss labeled as a "test."

I reached my truck and opened the door, slamming it harder than I should have.

WHEN TORNADOES COLLIDE

THE REST OF THE WEEK was somewhat boring; I didn't even get another glimpse of the president at the office.

Unless mentioning the fact that a man removed his deceased wife's ring became the most exciting headline to fill the news.

The mysterious woman who made the president take off his ring had yet to appear. I wondered if she really existed, as he seemed the same—always mysterious in his public appearances, attentive to his voters, but discreet about his personal life.

It seemed he was having a hectic week. I always liked to stay informed about our country's politics, which included Christopher Fitzgerald, so I kept track of his movements.

My phone rang as I sat on the sofa at home. I had just arrived from college; it was Friday, and I could go out and meet someone. But everything pointed to me ending up in bed, sleeping. That's what my mind wanted—rest.

"Hello?" I sighed into the phone.

"Hazel? This is Meg, from our art course." Yes, I knew who Meg was; we talked during class and breaks. She was one of the few classmates I had.

"Hi, Meg, of course I know who you are." I laughed because Meg could be a bit scatterbrained at times.

"I looked for you around campus today but didn't find you. We're going to a resort tomorrow; a bunch of us are going. Do you want to come? We're taking a van, which will be in the campus parking lot at six in the morning. Are you in?"

She sounded very excited, and I admitted that I was too. After a boring week, it would be nice to hang out with people my age, just drinking, having fun, and doing crazy things.

"Of course I'm in. Just tell me what I need to bring," I enthusiastically accepted the invitation.

CHAPTER EIGHTEEN

Hazel

The van ride lasted over two hours, and since it was very early, most people slept, including me. Meg had mentioned that there was an indoor heated pool and a bar where everyone could drink. It was an ideal place to spend the weekend.

I opened the curtain and saw the resort with a huge hotel in front. The van parked there.

"Let's wake up your sleepyheads, we've arrived." Meg clapped her hands excitedly.

She opened the door, and the light flooded in as everyone grabbed their backpacks. There were about ten of us—six women and four men. The fact that there were more women wasn't an issue for me, as I wasn't interested in hunting for men here.

In fact, I wasn't in the mood for sex, not after the craziness I'd experienced with Christopher—or what I thought I had experienced.

We entered the hotel. Beside me was a girl I didn't know; the only person I recognized was Meg. She was ahead, taking charge of everything.

I noticed some security guards dressed in black inside, and they whispered something into their microphones as they saw us stop there.

I stayed close to the front desk near Meg, listening as she said:

"We have a reservation for five rooms with the resort package." She sounded excited.

The receptionist confirmed the details; everything was in order. However, what caught my attention was what she said at the end.

"We have important guests here who are staying in the luxury area on the third floor, so under no circumstances are you allowed to go up there," she said firmly.

"Got it," Meg confirmed.

Our rooms were on the second floor. So Meg took the keys given to her. The weather outside wasn't ideal for the outdoor pool, so we might go to the indoor one.

We climbed the stairs, and on the second floor, there were also security guards. But who the hell was important enough to warrant that many guards?

"We're here," Meg pointed out the doors. "Okay, guys, am I the only one curious about who's staying here?"

She whispered as if she didn't want those guards, who were too far away to hear, to overhear what she said.

"It must be the president with his mysterious woman," the woman beside me said mockingly.

"I'd love to be the mysterious woman next to that man," another one sighed as she spoke.

"Shut up, do you really think mere mortals like you have a chance with a man like Christopher Fitzgerald? These powerful men can have any model they want," one of the guys scoffed, feeling pained by the girls' dreams of a powerful man.

"Meg, can we split up the rooms?" I spoke up, as my brother-in-law was a Fitzgerald and I wasn't in the mood to reveal that my sister was married to one of the powerful.

I couldn't stay silent and not defend my brother-in-law, and since I didn't want to do either, I quickly asked about the room assignments.

My personal life wasn't something I usually shared. I knew there were curious people who would ask what Zachary Fitzgerald was like in daily life, but that wasn't any of their business.

The rooms were assigned, and I ended up with Meg, which was a relief since she was the only person I knew.

"Hazel, how about we put on swimsuits and head to the indoor pool?" Meg clapped her hands excitedly.

"Sure, I just need to stop by the hotel restaurant first; I need a caffeine boost." I sat on the bed, rubbing my eyes.

"Okay, see you at the pool then." She didn't even change her clothes and quickly left the room.

I was left alone, frowning, wondering if she wasn't going to put on her swimsuit. Then the door opened again.

"I forgot I need to change clothes." It was impossible not to laugh at the woman who seemed to be in her own little world.

Meg, in her excitement, ended up changing before me. I took my time, putting on a bikini and then a long dress over it, leaving my hair loose.

I stopped in front of the mirror, just applying some lip gloss. The room was empty when I left the bathroom. I grabbed one of my small bags and left the room, leaving the only key inside because Meg had left in such a hurry she didn't even remember to leave the key with me.

I frowned when I noticed the movement on the stairs but stopped walking when the security guard made a gesture with his hand, blocking my path, which made me roll my eyes.

I stood there waiting to see who was coming down; at least I could satisfy the girls' curiosity and find out who was there.

"This can't be happening," I muttered to myself.

It seemed that my presence also caught his attention because the president turned his face, and our eyes met. What a crappy fate that kept putting me in his path?

Christopher, who appeared to be with that woman, stopped walking as if he wasn't thinking, just halting without considering that he might be noticed.

"Are you following me?" he said, a bit louder.

"I don't know if you realize, but this is a resort. I have much more important things in my life than to care about where the hell the president is," I retorted.

"So you're saying it's just a coincidence that we're in the same place?" It was clear that the woman beside him was paying close attention to everything.

"Blame fate because I had no idea I'd be here. Now, if your men will excuse me, I have friends waiting for me at the pool," I said, deciding not to go to the restaurant as it seemed likely they'd head there.

"Friends? Men?" *Seriously? Was he really asking that? Still with the whole men thing?*

"Yes, men, lots of men, and I'm the only woman. I'm going to have a blast," my voice came out more irritated than I expected. "Forget about me, Christopher!"

I called him by his first name, brushed past those security guards, and hurried down the damned stairs, eager to escape from that confusing man.

First, he ignored me every moment we were together, constantly dismissing my presence and my opinion. Suddenly he wanted to kiss me and now he seemed concerned about who I was with. I was getting confused, very confused.

CHAPTER NINETEEN

Hazel

I didn't know where the pool was. There were no doors in the back, so I wandered down the corridor, desperately looking for any door, but found nothing!

I heard footsteps behind me, but without stopping to look, I kept walking.

Until those large hands grabbed my wrist, pulling me *back*, shoving me roughly against a wall. He didn't even look at me as he opened a door next to us, apparently leading to some room.

"What do you think you're doing?" I asked as I entered what seemed to be a room.

The president pressed me against one of the walls, while our eyes met in the ambient light coming through the windows.

"Who do you think you are, challenging me in front of my security?" he growled, his hands still gripping my wrists.

"Me? You started with the story about following me when I was just heading to the pool..."

"With your friends!" he interrupted rudely.

"Yes, there are men, but I'd be with my friend, *friend*!" I emphasized the word "friend." "Not that it's any of your business since you're such a jerk."

Without thinking, when he released my wrists, I grabbed his jacket collar, trying to push him away.

"And what about Miller?"

"Why is that your concern? Why should I talk about my life?" Despite my resistance, Christopher moved his face closer to mine, as if my strength couldn't compete with his.

"*Hell*! Because I want you, damn it!!!" he roared as he pressed his body against mine, his large hands gripping my waist so tightly that I could even feel the pressure.

I had no time to say anything as his lips were attacking mine, nothing subtle or gentle. It was a fiery kiss.

Christopher didn't ask for permission as his tongue entered my mouth aggressively. I felt the exact moment it touched mine, sliding along it. My hands remained fixed between us, unable to move.

Even with such a voracious kiss, it was delicious, wet, not dry at all. I turned my head, making him almost devour my tongue.

The president's hand moved from my waist to between the wall and my buttocks, gripping it firmly. The thin fabric of my dress allowed me to feel each of his fingers on my butt.

Biting my lip, pulling it forcefully, he pulled his face away from mine. My head was tilted back, our eyes locked, and he blinked a few times before stepping back and removing his hands from me.

"Is this the moment you realize this is all a mistake and run away?" I asked in a whisper, trying to recover from the sudden attack.

"No, absolutely not a mistake." Christopher was breathing heavily—*but...*, *but...* I need to go, I need to think about this first, *I... I...*

He couldn't speak, seeming dazed, even stuttering.

"Christopher," I whispered his name.

"Don't be mad at me, but for now this is too much for me. I need to get out of here."

Turning abruptly, he left the room, leaving me alone. What did he mean by that? Too much?

Was my kiss not good? Did his deceased wife come to his mind? Oh God!

I spotted an armchair and sat in it, staying there for long minutes, not even knowing what to think of the situation. If I was confused before, now I was twice as much.

I got up from the armchair, gathered my bag that had fallen on the floor, and ran my hand over my lips, as if I could still feel him there, kissing me, touching me. Christopher kissed better than I expected, and to think I had set a good kiss for him in my thoughts.

I left the room, looking around, but finding no one. I retraced my steps down the stairs and found a gentleman in a hotel uniform, whom I asked for directions.

"Do you know where the indoor pool is?" I asked.

"Going out that door, just follow straight ahead and you'll find the indoor pool," he replied, and I thanked him with a smile.

I followed the route he described. It wasn't hard to find; it was in the opposite direction of where I had gone, which is why I hadn't found the pool in that corridor earlier.

Meg let out a squeal as soon as she saw me walking through the door. I went over to her, and it was impossible not to smile with her because she was a walking disaster, but always laughing and finding the bright side of life.

"Did you manage to go to the restaurant?" she asked right away.

"Oh, there were too many people, so I decided not to go." I smiled awkwardly.

I took off my dress, leaving it with Meg's clothes. My bag and phone too.

I sat on the edge of the pool watching one of the girls running towards us, excited, and as she walked, she was already taking off her denim shorts.

"You won't believe who I ran into on my way to the pool." She threw her clothes on top of ours.

Without sparing any effort, she jumped into the pool, splashing water everywhere. I turned my face, closed my eyes, and felt the droplets hit my face.

"Spit it out already, Lili," Meg complained about the delay.

"Calm down, impatient. I was making my grand entrance," she teased, splashing water at Meg.

"If I had known, I wouldn't have kept it to myself," Meg grumbled, shrugging her shoulders.

"I won't keep it, especially since anyone quick enough will see him at the restaurant; he just came in with all his men." Lili sighed loudly.

"Who, Lili?" Meg even deepened her voice.

"Our dream president, he's here in this very hotel. Can you *believe* it? Fitzgerald is right here." Her eyes seemed to drift off as if she were planning their wedding.

"Seriously, you didn't see him, Hazel?" Meg asked, and at that moment, I thought it best to lie.

"No, I just saw a bunch of people and left the restaurant. I'll have coffee another time." I smiled awkwardly, then jumped into the pool with them to enjoy the time.

CHAPTER TWENTY

Hazel

I left the pool with the girls, heading towards our room. I needed a shower, and then we'd figure out what to do next.

I took a slow shower and washed my hair. Since I didn't know what to wear, I would put on a robe for now, and then change into something once Meg decided what we'd do.

I sat on the bed when someone knocked on the door. Meg was in the shower, so I got up, went to the door, opened it, and saw a man standing there.

"Miss, this is for you." He handed me a single light-blue rose.

There was also a small envelope with it.

I thanked him for the delivery, closed the door, and held the envelope and rose in my hands, bringing the rose to my nose and smelling it gently. It was incredibly fragrant and delicate.

I sat on my bed, leaving the rose beside me. It was perfect; I had never seen such a beautiful one.

I opened the envelope and took out a small letter, reading it:

"I didn't know what your favorite flower was, so I sent a blue rose to match the color of your eyes. I hope you like it. Have dinner with me tonight; one of my security will pick you up at 8 PM. Don't tell anyone.

Affectionately, C. Fitzgerald."

He sent this? Was it Christopher who made this invitation? It was obviously him; the handwriting was his.

I stared at the note for several seconds until I heard the shower being turned off quickly. I put the letter back in the envelope, hid it under the pillow, opened the drawer next to the bed, and placed the rose there. That way, I wouldn't have to explain anything to Meg.

Meg came out of the bathroom wearing a robe just like mine.

"It sounded like someone knocked on the door," she said as she dried her hair.

"Just your imagination." I shrugged my shoulders.

"Oh," she didn't question further and went towards her bag. "I was thinking of going to the restaurant for an afternoon drink. What do you think?"

We had had lunch by the pool, ordering some snacks and eating there. After receiving that note, I thought the last thing my stomach could handle was more food, especially since I was extremely eager for that dinner.

"You can go without me. I'm sure the girls will want to go." I smiled sideways.

"Aren't you hungry?" she asked, frowning.

"Actually, I want to check out an antique shop I saw here at the hotel." I got up from my bed, opening my bag.

"*Oh*, alright then." She did the same, opening her bag on her bed.

We chose our clothes, and without much conversation, we each got dressed. I put on jeans and a white shirt.

I let Meg leave first, carefully putting the letter and the flower back in my bag.

I wasn't going to an accessory shop but rather the clothing store in the hotel. I needed something to wear for that dinner; I hadn't brought any clothes for such an occasion, so I was looking for something.

I left the room; the president's security was no longer there, which meant Christopher had likely left. But what intrigued me the most was the fact that he was in the same hotel.

I took out my phone to look for information about the presidency but found nothing useful. He was probably there for a business meeting.

I went down the stairs, walked through the lobby, and exited the hotel, finding the two shops outside. One for clothes and one for decorative accessories.

I stopped at the window, pursed my lips upon seeing that there was apparently nothing suitable for a dinner with the president. I wondered why I wanted to look so nice for a man who had disregarded me several times.

Unless I wanted to show him what he had missed by judging me as just a bold woman; I was much more than that.

Knowing that this was my only choice, I went into the store, and as soon as I walked through the door, the saleswoman came over to me.

"How can I help you?" She clasped her hands, being helpful.

"I'm looking for a dress for a dinner, and some shoes as well," I said while looking around.

"I believe I have something." She motioned for me to follow her.

We stopped in front of a rack. There were many dresses, mostly floral, but not in the style I wanted.

There was only one in a solid color that I immediately picked up. The color was a dark gray, not the type of color I'd choose for a first date, but it was the only option I had, and it was the best in my size.

"I'll take this one," I said, looking at the tag and noting that it was within my budget.

"Would you like to try it on, dear?"

"No need." I shook my head and moved towards the shoes.

"What's your size?"

When I told her my size, she started showing me different styles. At least there were more options there.

I chose a pair of heels, paid at the register, and the woman thanked me. She probably didn't have many customers, as she seemed very excited about the sale.

I went back to my room, now needing to come up with a lie for Meg. Even though Christopher had made it clear not to tell anyone, I wouldn't say a word.

I knew how these things worked; I had seen how my sister was labeled as a gold-digger when her relationship with Zachary was revealed. The media was often ruthless, not caring if it hurt others.

Savannah went through hell before finally being loved by the media and the public. It took long days for her to be accepted. Luckily, Zachary didn't let any of it affect her.

I hid my purchase. With some help from fate, Meg would go somewhere, and I wouldn't have to explain why I bought new clothes.

I didn't want to mention receiving an invitation from a man because if I did, Meg would want to know who he was, and I'd have to come up with another lie. I preferred to stay silent.

CHAPTER TWENTY-ONE

Hazel

Just as he had said, at 8 PM, one of his security guards knocked on my door.

Meg had gone out; she and the others went to a nearby nightclub, and since I had claimed I wanted to go to bed early, it was easy to come up with an excuse, saying that a migraine had hit me hard.

"Miss Bellingham, if you could come with me," the security guard said as soon as I appeared at the door.

We walked down the hallway, and I considered that he might be taking me to a reserved spot in the restaurant, but the place I was guided to was on the third floor.

Heading towards the luxury area, the tall man knocked on a door, speaking into his earpiece. After a few seconds, he allowed me to pass.

Nervously, I entered the hotel room, and to my surprise, it wasn't just a room; it had a sitting area with a lovely table set with two candles in metal holders.

Movement came from the side as my eyes caught the president rising from the bed where he had been sitting, tucking his cell phone into his pants pocket.

"Hello," I whispered as our eyes met.

"You came." He frowned in an amusing way.

"Are you kidding? Missing a dinner with the President of the United States?" I dramatically placed my hand over my heart.

"If you didn't keep teasing me, I'd almost believe in this brief bout of fandom." Christopher didn't come towards me or greet me with a kiss.

"If you could, I'd like your autograph. I've already kept the letter to show my future granddaughters," I continued my act. "Look, my dear, Grandma received a letter from the President of our country."

I mimicked an elderly lady holding a cane, managing to get a smile out of the president.

"I pity your husband." He pulled out a chair for me to sit.

"That's not necessary; he will be a lucky man," I teased, moving closer to him.

"You speak with such conviction." He raised an eyebrow subtly.

"Of course, I know I'm a good catch. I know how to win my candidacy," I declared without sitting, standing in front of him, and as soon as our eyes met. "Don't you greet the people you dine with?"

"Actually, I think I'm a bit rusty in that department," he whispered, not taking his eyes off my lips.

"You can start now." I moistened my lips.

Christopher lowered his face, not touching me with his hands, his lips lightly brushing my forehead.

"I don't want to lose focus; let's have dinner." He stepped back, and with a sigh, I sat down in my chair.

Christopher sat at the head of the table, and I beside him. The table was set for only two people.

As soon as we were seated, two women appeared, each with a tray.

I said nothing, simply waiting for my plate to be placed in front of me. A man appeared with a bottle of wine, filling Christopher's glass and then mine.

As soon as we were alone, slow music started playing in the background, so softly it was barely noticeable.

"Did you tell anyone about our meeting?" he asked, bringing his glass to his lips.

"Did you forget that my sister is married to your cousin and everything she went through? You didn't even need to ask; I wouldn't tell anyone," I said sensibly.

"You're right, I forgot about that," he replied, not continuing the conversation.

I waited for him to speak, but Christopher started eating, so I did the same, eating in silence while curiosity nearly ate me alive, wanting to ask a million questions.

"You're quiet," he finally said, setting his utensils beside his plate.

"Actually, I'm quite curious." I gave a small smile.

"You'd be quite frustrated if you weren't curious." The president took a sip from his glass.

"So, I can be what you call invasive?" I provoked him as I made my request.

"You're completely free to be, just ask that what we talk about stays between us." He didn't take his eyes off me.

"Do you trust me to reveal sordid secrets of your life?"

"Who said I'm going to reveal sordid secrets?" He raised an eyebrow mockingly.

"I know how to extract great information." I shrugged, confident.

"A good strategy for a future lawyer."

"I'm learning from the best," he understood I was referring to his mother.

Our plates of food were finished.

"Go ahead, ask your question. What's the one that's pulsing most in your thoughts?" he asked, and I gave a sideways smile.

"There are so many, but I'll start with the first one." I bit the corner of my lip, looking at his empty fingers. "Why did you take off your wedding ring? I want to know much more than what you said to the newspapers..."

"I didn't say anything concrete to them," he cut me off.

"That's why I want a complete answer."

"I took it off because I felt it was the moment," he replied, making a face at his answer.

"No, Mr. President, I want much more than that." I rolled my eyes.

"When I tried to kiss you at the beach house, it made me realize that I hadn't done that with any other woman, only with you, and having the ring on my finger felt like betraying my wife..."

"Deceased, she's no longer alive. It doesn't make me seem like the other woman; you are a widower," I interrupted him, as he spoke as if that woman were still alive.

"That's right, that was the reason. There's nothing more behind why I took off the ring." We were interrupted by the women who came to clear our plates.

I waited for them to leave, finishing my wine and moistening my lips immediately afterward.

"And why me?" I seized the moment to ask a new question.

"I don't know; I ask myself the same question, and all that comes to mind is why not you?" He flashed a small smile.

The women returned, bringing with them new trays of desserts.

"Dessert." My eyes lit up at the sight of a small dish containing something resembling chocolate.

"Dessert couldn't be missed." He made me glance briefly in his direction and then back to the sweet treat that I began eating almost immediately.

"I love sweets," I murmured like a child.

"I noticed." Even after receiving his dessert, he didn't eat it, as if it were more intriguing to watch me.

CHAPTER TWENTY-TWO

Hazel

I finished my dessert, and Christopher hadn't even touched his.

"You ordered two desserts but didn't eat yours?" I asked.

He raised his hand as I watched his movement. I ran my thumb along the corner of my lip and wiped something that was there.

"You left a little trace of chocolate here." The president's eyes fixed on my lip.

"Aren't you going to eat your dessert?" I asked again, as the little sweet tooth that I was.

"I know a better way to eat it." He ran the tip of his finger along his lip, subtly licking what he had picked up from my mouth.

"Definitely, that way is much more pleasant to the eyes," I whispered, thrilled by the scene.

Christopher extended his hand, and I took it as he gently dragged his chair back, causing me to sit sideways on his lap, my face aligned with his.

One of his hands was on my back.

"By the way, you look incredibly beautiful tonight," he whispered.

"You don't have to lie." I rolled my eyes.

"I'm not lying; you're beautiful." He tucked my hair behind my ear.

"The hotel store didn't have anything even remotely appropriate for a dinner with the president." I made a face.

"You bought this outfit just to come here?"

"Yeah, I didn't bring much clothing; after all, we're heading back tomorrow." I casually poured wine into my empty glass.

"You shouldn't have bought it; if I had known, I would have sent something for you to wear." He looked at me with concern.

"If you had done that, I would have felt like a high-class woman." I lifted my glass to my lips; that rich wine was delicious.

"You would never be." He winked as his fingers touched my neck.

Christopher was analyzing every part of my face, as if marking every little corner. He wasn't the type of man who would immediately pounce on a woman; he seemed to be cooking her slowly.

"The rose you sent is beautiful," I said, remembering the lovely blue rose.

"It matches your eyes." He was almost begging for one of those kisses he had given me earlier.

"I assume you haven't told your cousin anything?"

"I'd prefer if no one in my family knew," I nodded, as I preferred the same.

Remembering that he wore the necklace with his wife's ring, I raised my hand and touched his chest, a little below his neck, knowing that the ring should be there.

"Did you take it off?" I asked when he realized what I was looking for.

"How did you know I wore it?" He squinted.

"Once it showed over your shirt when you bent down in the office; it's not something only a few people knew." I shrugged.

"Yes, I took it off; I no longer carry anything of hers with me." Christopher didn't even glance away, noticing the anguish in his eyes every time she was mentioned.

"It's no use removing all of that if your thoughts are still on her," I ended up saying without thinking, a bit jealous.

Christopher said nothing; I tried to get up from his lap, a movement I managed with ease, heading toward his bed, in the part that was his room, and turned around to hear his footsteps coming toward me.

"This year marks twelve years since I lost her. I never imagined I could endure such pain; it felt as if Anna had taken a part of me with her. Believe me, if I invited you to this dinner, it's because something inside me reignited, something that hadn't happened in twelve years of my life. I took off the rings because I felt in my heart that it was a betrayal, both to you and to her. I will never compare you two." He continued walking and stopped in front of me. "Don't expect that being with me will involve sex; that is out of the question. I am not like the men you are used to dating. For years I lived in celibacy, and if I am here with you, don't make me want to rush..."

His hands touched my waist, pulling me closer to him, and my face was lifted toward his.

"You could have made a bet with Savannah; I would have won easily," I mocked his situation.

"What's the problem with that?"

"Tell me, sir, since every time I asked, you avoided the question." I raised my hand, touching his neck and scratching it with the tips of my fingers.

"My sex life is no one's business." He shrugged nonchalantly.

"Do you know how to engage in sexual activity?" I bit the corner of my lip, mocking the situation.

"Of course I do." A little squeak escaped my mouth as Christopher effortlessly lifted me onto his lap.

He laid me down on the bed while his body covered mine, not pressing me as his face covered the curve of my neck, leaving wet kisses there, and I closed my eyes, feeling him.

Slowly, he moved up, touching my chin and stopping above my mouth.

"You're so beautiful," he whispered, giving me a lingering kiss. "When you're like this, you even seem harmless; I wouldn't guess you're the same woman who constantly teases me."

"I must confess I love teasing you," I murmured, opening my eyes and finding his face there.

Christopher had smooth skin, a sign of a man who shaves regularly, a small dimple on his chin, so tiny it barely attracted attention, and his black eyebrows matched his eyelashes, contrasting with the extremely blue color of his eyes.

"Is this some kind of fetish?" The president furrowed his brow in a funny way.

"It could be, but it's not. It's just that you're so easy to rattle; you have the political version, always impartial, never losing your cool, but whenever you're with your family, where you can be yourself, oh, in those moments, you're so easy to rattle." I let out a soft laugh.

"How did you notice that?" He seemed genuinely interested.

"Even before Savannah got together with Zachary, I was already very interested in everything related to politics, and I would sit next to my dad watching TV, asking him to explain things to me. You met my dad at Sav's wedding; he's a bit obsessed." I remembered my sister's wedding, where my dad practically threw himself into the poor president's arms.

"Yes, I remember him very well." Christopher made a face.

"I knew your political side very well through the newspapers I read or the digital news, and I just connected it with the other side of your daily life, starting with our first meeting at Zachary's house in California; your look at me was deadly." It was impossible not to laugh remembering that day.

"You know you have a terrible habit of wanting to fix everything, even where it's not necessary."

"Yes, it's my weakness; I'll protect anyone who's by my side. I come from a flamboyant family; we tend to attract attention wherever we go, only Savannah is the exception." My eyes caught his finger sliding over the fabric of my dress.

"I think I can get used to your weakness," he hadn't said I needed to change, but rather that he wanted to get used to my weakness.

CHAPTER TWENTY-THREE

Christopher

I wanted to spend the night with those beautiful blue eyes beside me, but I couldn't forget Sydney's words: "Have dinner with the girl, and at 10 PM I'll be in your room to discuss the agenda for your upcoming rally in support of the homeless in Chicago."

It was a project that Governor Malcolm Beaumont had been demanding some action on from me. Finally, we had made it a priority.

I checked my wristwatch and saw that we still had half an hour together.

"Are you looking at the clock because you're kicking me out of your room?" The little one held onto my shoulder.

"Actually, I have an appointment with my assistant at 10 PM. It was supposed to be earlier, but I asked her to reschedule for later." I slid my fingers down Hazel's slightly flushed cheek.

"Your assistant must hate me now," she had a way of making light of everything.

"Actually, Sydney is probably at the bar singing to some woman right now." I moved off Hazel's small body and sat on my bed.

"Seriously? Your assistant likes the same fruit as you? And I could have sworn she had a crush on you," she loved mixing the formal with the informal in her speech.

"Sydney likes women more than I do," I joked about the situation.

"So, she even eats the pit of the fruit you like." I burst into laughter; it was the first time someone had said that in my presence.

"Exactly." Noticing that she sat on the bed, I pulled her into my arms and ran my hand down her legs, sliding her heels off the floor.

"For a man living in celibacy, you sure know how to easily get a woman's shoe off." Hazel provocatively sat on my lap and placed a leg on each side of my waist.

The dress lifted, and even though she gathered the fabric in the middle of her legs, it didn't stop me from seeing her tanned legs as my fingers began to tingle, needing that moment, needing to have my hand on her skin.

"Hazel, you little tease," I whispered, lifting my eyes from her thigh, her lips curled in a sidelong smile.

"You can touch me, President, I don't bite," her voice was husky, like a sex nymph, she knew how to provoke.

If it were any other woman in her place, I wouldn't get the effect she had on me. It was as if I desired only her, only Hazel.

"I'm afraid to start and not be able to stop," I murmured, gripping the bed sheet tightly.

"Not stopping is something I would also enjoy." Her delicate fingers touched mine as I held the sheet.

Hazel made me release it, guiding my hand to her bare thigh. I felt her soft, smooth, delicate skin, contrasting with my own tone, which was lighter compared to her delicious tan, and with a bit of force, I squeezed her.

"Mmm..." a loud sigh escaped her mouth, my eyes fixed on her slightly parted lips. "I like being squeezed."

"You do?" I asked impulsively.

"Actually, I've never found a man who was rougher; it always felt like something was missing, I always wanted more, and left frustrated most of the time," she said, letting out another sigh as my hands moved up, nearing that dangerous curve, where I knew would be the limit of my perdition.

"In general... well, I used to be quite rough, more into a sex that was..." I trailed off, trying to find an exact definition.

"Wild?"

"I think that's about right." My fingers found her lace panties, feeling it at the tips of my fingers. "Damn it!"

As if I had burned myself, I pulled my hand away and widened my eyes as I met hers.

"Did I cross your limit?" she whispered, scared. "I've never heard you swear."

"You'd better get used to it then, and I hope you're not disappointed," I said, tucking her hair behind her ear.

"I'm looking forward to getting to know your depraved side." She bit the corner of her lips, then ran her tongue around her mouth in a slow and sensual way.

It was becoming difficult to control myself, keeping my member inert against the temptations beside Hazel. It had always been easy; I had become a master at it. But with that little tease, I felt my cock semi-erect in my pants, and if I got up at that moment, it would definitely be noticeable.

"Miss Bellingham," I whispered her name, pulling her closer to me, pressing her chest against mine.

"Mr. Fitzgerald," her husky voice was like a godsend.

"Are you leaving tomorrow?" I asked softly.

"Yes," she confirmed.

"Tomorrow I'm going to Chicago; I'll be there for a week. But when I come back, I want you in my house." I needed her, I craved her curves.

"You know it's not that simple, right? You can't just say you want me in your house and expect me to come running." Her face pulled away from mine.

"So, what should I do?" I asked curiously.

"First, you need to ask for my phone number, schedule a date at your place, and if I'm free, I'll accept." I frowned in confusion.

"And why wouldn't you be free? Do you prefer being with another man instead of me?" Jealousy was quickly rising in my mind.

"Calm down, Mr. President, I didn't mention other men. I'm just explaining how things work. Have they told you that you're quite jealous?" She let out a soft laugh.

"Hazel, my biggest flaw is jealousy. I have a tendency to take care of and spoil what's mine. All of this to have you by my side. I can't stand seeing another man looking at curves that belong to me. And you're mine; my body has claimed yours. I confess I'm starting to go a bit crazy with jealousy," I told her the truth.

"I've noticed that. For now, we don't need to worry about it," she whispered.

I spotted my phone nearby, picked it up, and asked her to write down her number. I would do as Hazel asked, send her a message, and we'd arrange our meeting.

CHAPTER TWENTY-FOUR

Hazel

A week had passed, and I hadn't heard from Christopher. He hadn't sent a message, and even if I had his number, I wouldn't have reached out. So, I continued with my routine of college and work, waiting for Friday to come around again.

My phone rang beside my desk, and I saw my sister's name on the screen, so I decided to answer the call:

"Sister?" Sav immediately spoke up.

"Yes?" I put the tip of my pen in my mouth, waiting for her to say what she wanted.

"Tomorrow, Zachary has an event. There will be many politicians, including Malcolm Beaumont, and he's a hottie."

"I bet Zachary isn't standing next to you listening to what you're saying," I teased.

"Details my husband doesn't need to hear. He'll always be my hottest." I heard her giggle. "Come with us. Scarlett is in town; she'll love spending time with you."

"I love that Scarlett is in town; that's the only reason I'll accept." Scarlett was Zach's younger sister, the only girl in the family.

Out of all the cousins, Scarlett was the only girl. Like their little gem, everyone protected her, the little darling of the Fitzgeralds.

"Come over to our house after your class today, so we can do some shopping tomorrow morning and visit a beauty salon," Savannah asked excitedly.

"Great, my hair needs a good treatment at the salon." I smiled, running my hand through my hair.

We ended the call on an excited note since we'd be spending the night together, or rather, I'd be spending it with my goddaughter.

I would leave the office and grab a change of clothes at home, keeping them for when I went to my sister's house.

"GODMOTHER, GODMOTHER" Sadie's enthusiastic voice woke me up.

We had a very long night; my goddaughter only saw me arriving at her house and lost any trace of sleep.

Since I couldn't say no to her, I ended up spending most of my night watching movies with my little one.

Silly me, thinking Sadie would fall asleep in the middle of the movie, a fact that didn't happen.

Slowly, I opened my eyes, finding the little one jumping on the bed. Her messy blonde hair and sleepy blue eyes showed she had just woken up.

"Hello, my angel." I sat up on the bed, picking her up in my arms and tickling her.

The bedroom door opened, and Savannah walked in, laughing at the sight of our mess.

"I see you two woke up quite cheerful," my sister said. "Come on, let's have breakfast. Mommy, godmother, and Aunt Scar are going out, and Grandma will come here to stay with you."

"Yay, Grandma!" Sadie jumped off the bed.

I got out of bed, running my hand through my hair and tying it up in a bun.

"You can go ahead; I'll change my clothes and get ready to face a day at the mall."

Savannah and Sadie left the room, and I stayed alone, grabbing my backpack from the floor.

I chose my jeans, a tank top, and quickly changed into them before heading to the bathroom to wash my face.

My stomach rumbled, indicating that I was very hungry.

I went back to the room, picked up my phone from the bed, and saw a notification. I unlocked the device, realizing the message was from an unsaved number. I opened it, reading a message from someone I least expected to hear from.

"*Said to send something when I was going out to dinner, are you available tonight?*"

Wow, seriously?

He had gone a week without talking to me, and when he did, it was like that? As if I were obligated to go out with him, the use of the word *available* was so subjective.

"*No, Christopher, I'm not available for you, and maybe I never will be!*"

I was blunt in my message and put my phone back in my pocket.

I left the room, going down the stairs, and while I heard my nieces' joyful laughter, I entered the breakfast room, finding it fully set.

Zachary, Savannah, little Alexis in her stroller making some sounds, Sadie sitting in her chair, accompanied by Grace, Zachary's mother, and Scarlett, his sister.

Scar spotted me, got up from her chair, came towards me, and gave me a tight hug. She was taller than me, and with heels, she became even taller.

"I missed you so much, Hazel," Scar said in her soft voice. She had been raised in all this luxury, exuding delicacy and elegance in every part of her being.

"I feel the same; this college life isn't easy," I joked amid the hug.

She was studying at Harvard, and we were almost the same age.

"Don't even get me started; I can't wait for all this to be over." We both laughed as we pulled away. "Come on, let's eat; we need to be well-fed for a day at the mall."

Clapping her hands, Scar took my hand, and then we headed to the table. I pulled my phone out of my pocket.

Before starting to eat, I saw Christopher's message:

"*What's wrong? What's the problem? What did I do wrong?*"

I sighed deeply and didn't reply to his message. I focused on the cheerful breakfast with the Fitzgerald family. They might be as snobbish as possible, but they were humble and enjoyed good conversation.

"Is Chris back in town?" Scarlett asked while everyone was eating.

"Yes, he arrived the previous night," Zachary answered.

He was back, sent a message only when he arrived in town, not even asking how my day had been, nothing, absolutely nothing!

And when he did return, it was with just a brief message of *available*?

"I hope he's not at the event. No one deserves that grumpy man," I replied.

"Well, it looks like he will be; he's one of the most anticipated guests," Zachary said.

I just rolled my eyes, knowing that I would see the president that night.

CHAPTER TWENTY-FIVE

Hazel

The day at the mall was hectic. Savannah made me try on several dresses until we decided what I would wear that night.

From what I understood, the event that evening would be attended by all the powerful politicians, who would brag about who had the most assets. *Of course, that wasn't the case,* but in my mind, that was the point of these parties.

What helped me unwind was when we sat in those salon chairs because as soon as I sat down, I relaxed.

Our hair and makeup were done at the salon, so when we got home, all that was left was to get dressed.

I was sharing the car with Scarlett on the way to the event, and she seemed somewhat apprehensive.

"Is everything okay, Scar?" I asked, unable to hide my curiosity.

"Oh, yes," she cleared her throat as she spoke.

"You seem off." I frowned.

"*Okay, okay,* promise to keep it a secret?"

"I'm a tomb." I mimed locking my lips.

"It's Malcolm; he's going to be there." Our eyes met in the dim light of the car, Scar fiddling with her fingers, impatient.

"Yes, he will be there," I wanted her to keep talking, so I stayed silent.

"I slept with him, well, we slept together." A forced laugh escaped her lips. "The best sex of my life, but I don't think it was the best for him, as he simply forgot me. Malcolm showed up in every magazine with some model, always with a different one. As if he was throwing in my face that what we had was awful. And now, I don't even know how to look him in the eyes. I'm so embarrassed..."

"*Oh, wow.* I wasn't expecting that," I gasped. "Do you want my help?"

"How could you help me?" She bit her lip.

"I can go talk to him if you want." I shrugged nonchalantly.

"But do you know him?" Scar looked at me as if I were completely crazy.

"Actually, no. I'm what they call good at making friends; I might get something out of the Governor of Illinois." I gave her my best mischievous smile.

"You're crazy, Hazel, *but..., but...* what if he hits on you?" She became apprehensive again.

"We'll know he's not good enough for you. But as for that, don't worry, I'd never be with a man who's been with my friend." I winked.

"Thanks, being raised as the family's little princess didn't prepare me for this kind of situation." Scar slumped her shoulders.

"If you want my opinion on what to do in these cases, it would be to make him jealous, but that's just me, a bit crazy. In your case, just ignore him and show how elegant you are, without caring about his opinion."

"Yes, first I want to find out what he thinks; if the response is negative, I'll do what I do best, be elegant without caring." Scarlett shrugged.

"Since you've shared a secret of yours, I'll share one of mine. I had dinner with your cousin Christopher; he said he wanted to see me again and used the word available in a way I hated. He had my number and only messaged me on the day he wanted to know if I was available." I rolled my eyes as I said the word a second time.

Scarlett's eyes widened first, then she cleared her throat before finally speaking:

"Christopher, we're talking about the same Christopher? The president? My cousin?"

"Yes, the very one." I burst into loud laughter.

"Sorry, the issue isn't with you but with him. I thought he was destined to die a widower." Suddenly, she burst into laughter. "But how was the dinner? Did anything happen?"

"Your cousin is too much of a gentleman to do anything, but he's got game; I wondered what it would be like to spend a night in those strong arms. We just kissed." I shrugged. "And the damn guy kisses well."

"Now that's a surprise. Chris with a woman. Wait, weren't you supposed to hate each other?"

"Actually, yes. I don't know if what we have is based on that hate. Your cousin is too straight-laced, an extremely attractive square. When we're alone, he doesn't even seem like the annoying man; I enjoyed being with him, getting to know this other side of him." I smiled, remembering our dinner, which didn't last long. "It's strange because he's so busy, he doesn't have time for anything."

"Maybe because he's the president of the country?" Scarlett furrowed her brow in an amusing way.

"Yes, but am I being unreasonable to think he should have at least sent a message during the week? Our dinner was last week, and he sent one single message yesterday, asking if I was available. Seriously? It feels like I'm just his plaything," I complained.

"Hazel, he knows you. He knows you're bold, a future lawyer full of arguments, and unlike Chris, you know how modern relationships work, not like him who's been in mourning for 12 years. So no, you're not wrong. It's your perspective, don't change it; he needs to adapt to you." She winked.

"You know you're an excellent counselor."

"I just don't follow my own advice." She gave a forced laugh.

The car slowed down, and we stopped in front of the massive event, where even a red carpet had been rolled out for the arriving guests.

The door opened, and I got out first, soon followed by Scar. A few flashes were fired in our direction, not many, as we weren't the most anticipated guests.

We moved inside the venue, the corridor was all lit up with lights, and the reception was excellent; they didn't ask for our names, probably recognizing the Fitzgerald face beside me.

The entire hall was decorated in shades of gray. A huge chandelier hung in the middle of what seemed to be a dance floor, where no one was dancing, while an orchestra played a slow, somewhat melancholic symphony, or maybe it was just me who didn't appreciate that type of music.

Scarlett linked her arm with mine as we headed toward our family, spotting my sister who had arrived before us.

CHAPTER TWENTY-SIX

Hazel

We stopped next to our family. Scarlett sat beside her mother while I stood next to my brother-in-law, who had his hand on my sister's waist.

The movement in front of us made me lift my eyes, noticing who was approaching: Christopher next to the Governor of Illinois. I didn't hold his gaze; in fact, I kept my attention well away from the president.

I could feel the tension in the air as if he were watching me, like tiny ants crawling over my body. Even without exchanging a look, I felt his gaze, intensely fixed on me.

Zachary soon struck up a conversation with the two men who arrived. Scarlett, sitting next to her mother, tried to attract the Governor's attention. She played with her hair, tossing it back, fidgeting with her fingers—small, pointless movements, as Malcolm wasn't looking at her.

Malcolm was a handsome man, completely the opposite of the Fitzgeralds in terms of looks: jet-black hair and eyes, tanned skin, as if he lived in the sun, but it was clearly his natural tone.

It was hard to keep my eyes off the president when he looked impeccably handsome; it was hard for that man to ever look unattractive.

"I didn't know you were in town, Scar," Christopher said, looking at Scarlett.

"Yes, Mom invited me. I missed my family." It was at that brief moment I saw Malcolm looking at Scar, but he quickly looked away as if out of obligation.

"I'm going to take a walk," Malcolm said in a normal tone, making sure everyone heard him.

"Oh, may I join you?" I asked a bit louder; it was an opportunity to clear up that situation and maybe spark a bit of jealousy in the president.

Before he responded, Malcolm glanced quickly at Scarlett.

"Yes, of course." He nodded.

I gave a brief smile, but with the intent of affecting Christopher, I lifted my gaze. The president had his attention fixed on me, as if he were glaring at me.

I stepped away from the table, walking alongside Malcolm.

"I know about your reputation, Miss Bellingham," he said beside me.

"What reputation am I not aware of?" I lifted my gaze as if I were an innocent girl.

"You like to draw attention wherever you go, and more importantly, I know about him." I narrowed my eyes.

"Who exactly are we talking about?" I needed to be sure we were talking about the same person.

"Chris," Malcolm was direct. "He told me since he couldn't confide in his cousins because we all know they'd get involved in your case."

Yes, the Fitzgeralds were the type of family that meddled in each other's lives, believing they were the best.

"Well, I also know about you and her." I shrugged, accepting a glass of champagne from a passing waiter.

"You do, huh?" The governor gave a small smile.

"Yes, and believe me, I'm quite curious to know what happened." I took a small sip from my glass.

"Was she the one who sent you?" We stopped walking; we were at a good distance from the table.

"Yes, actually no, I volunteered to find out what happened; I'm quite curious, you know." I gave a mocking smile.

"I'm noticing, but no one can know about this," he was somewhat rude in his reprimand.

"I won't tell. But you know how Scarlett is; after all, she practically grew up with Zoey. Why did you do this to her? Why play with her feelings? If you didn't want anything serious, why not go out with any other woman? Now she's thinking the problem is with her. And we know Scar is too beautiful, polite, and delicate; there's nothing about her that's a problem," I said directly.

"Is she feeling guilty?" Malcolm now seemed curious.

"Yes, Scarlett is too good. The other men she was involved with before you were all her age. Now she kind of fell in love." I handed my empty glass to the passing waiter and took another full one.

"It shouldn't have happened; she shouldn't be feeling this way," Malcolm whispered somewhat apprehensively.

"So, you're going to be the galaxy's big shot one night and the next pretend you don't even know her?" He shook his head at what I had said.

"When Christopher said you were a work of nature, he was right. I'll find a way to talk to Scarlett and clear these doubts with her."

"Seriously? I won't find out anything?" I pouted my lips.

"Curiosity killed the cat, you know?" The governor gave a small smile.

"What do you think you're doing?" The growl beside me startled me, as I hadn't seen him there.

"Talking? Normal people talk and converse with each other," I said with a hint of mockery in my voice.

"Brother, nothing happened, just talking about my sister," Malcolm lied, dragging his sister into it. "You know I would never be a busybody."

"That's not what it looks like," Christopher growled, stepping toward Malcolm.

"Stop the madness, brother..."

A new person approached, and I recognized her as Christopher's assistant. We had never been formally introduced, but I had seen her several times.

"Is there a problem?" she asked immediately.

"Everyone, your little toy there thinks he can put a leash on me," I retorted, narrowing my eyes at Christopher.

"We had an agreement," he whispered.

"That agreement must have existed only in your mind." I rolled my eyes.

"Hazel, don't provoke me!"

"Let's stop this little whispering theater; you're starting to attract attention," the assistant interjected.

"We need to talk," Christopher said seriously.

"Don't you want to see if I'm even *available* first?" I mocked.

"What's the problem? Are you going to explain it or not?"

"You, Christopher, stay away for the week, don't send me a single message, and when you come back, you think I'm obliged to be available for you?" I unloaded.

With that, I left. Now he knew the reason for my behavior, and it would have to be up to him to take the next step to fix this mess.

Asking for a message during the week wasn't too much to ask, was it?

CHAPTER TWENTY-SEVEN

Christopher

"Christopher, what's going on? I'm helping you with this relationship, but if you don't tell me what's happening, I won't be able to assist you," Sydney said as soon as we were alone.

My assistant had supported our "relationship" from the beginning, as she called it. Sydney, being a helpful person who loved to assist me with everything, wanted to know all the details.

"I sent her a message yesterday, a simple message, but it seems it wasn't what Hazel expected, which is strange since I'm usually good at everything I do," I complained, watching her extend her hand for me to show her the message, since I hadn't shown it to her.

Sydney read the message. She furrowed her brow, pushing it up, seeing that there was nothing more, just that single message.

"Clearly, your talent for relationships is rusty, Chris. You don't send her anything all week, and when you do, you ask if she's available? Nothing against the word, it was the way you used it. If it were any other woman, it might have worked, but we're talking about your cousin's wife's sister, someone who is practically part of your family. She knows you well enough to accept only that. You'll need a lot more than a message to get her attention." Sydney handed the phone back to me.

"Did I do it wrong, then?" I put the phone back inside my jacket.

"I wouldn't say wrong." My assistant frowned. "But you need to understand that not all women will kneel at your feet."

I nodded thoughtfully; that wasn't my intention. I had a very hectic week in Springfield with Malcolm, but that didn't stop me from thinking about her; my thoughts were entirely on Hazel. That little troublemaker, without asking for permission, had taken over all my thoughts. It was even strange since, since Anna was gone, she was the first to achieve such a feat.

I didn't feel guilty; thinking about Hazel wasn't a mistake. I knew Anna was gone, and our marriage would never return. Not like a marriage that ended in divorce; she was gone, my wife would never come back, and although it had hurt a lot for many years, Hazel was like a balm in my life, and I didn't know how far this could go.

"Do you know where she went?" I asked Sydney.

"No, I didn't see, but the President has a speech to give now; there's no time to chase after your girl." She rolled her eyes.

We had always been good friends; there was no real reason to hide things from her. Sydney knew more about me than my own family.

"Alright," I nodded, heading towards the stage in front of the dance floor, where a singer would soon perform.

Leona Brins was a contemporary singer known for her slow pop rhythm. I knew this from the speech I had memorized for that night.

Zachary approached me, and we went up the three flights of stairs together.

"What happened with my sister-in-law? Were you arguing again?" he whispered next to me.

"How do you know we argued?" I murmured without looking at him.

"It's not necessary to hear; I saw the two of you from afar with the same expressions you have when arguing." I turned my face towards Zachary as he squinted his eyes at me, and it was clear that my cousin saw Hazel as a sister.

"It wasn't anything major; I just didn't like seeing her talking to Malcolm." Zachary looked suspicious of what I had just said.

"Funny, since you never cared about that before." He narrowed his eyes at me.

"Yeah, but now I care." I shrugged.

"How so?" Zachary grabbed my elbow as we approached the microphone, standing behind the wooden pillar with the Washington DC flag symbol on it, the microphone mounted there.

"We can talk about this later; I ended up talking too much." I grumbled without diverting my eyes from my cousin.

"No way, you're seeing my sister-in-law, and you're..."

"No, Zach, nothing is happening as you might be imagining," I was direct so he wouldn't misunderstand "just don't tell your wife yet."

"No sex?" Zach said so quietly that his voice came out as a whisper, but I extended what I had said.

"None." I tapped the microphone to check if it was on.

With that, I considered my conversation with Zachary over, knowing he'd want to know more when we came down.

"Good evening," I said in a normal voice, hearing it come out loud through the microphone. "Thank you to everyone present at this event, which is important for the politics of our country. We will have an intense week in parliament; we'll decide on the most urgent matters from each state. The funds allocated for this week are in line with what we expected; we can make this week of great achievements."

The event aimed to secure additional funding for each state, called a state drive. Each governor would prioritize a case that wasn't within their budget, an extra benefit for their state.

"And as a guest, we have tonight, Leona Brins," I continued, pointing to the stairs where the woman was ascending. She was tall, wearing a sparkling dress, and immediately directed a smile at me, as all women did, seeming as though her eyes were shining in my direction. "Welcome, Miss Leona."

I spoke only to her, holding her hand as a greeting, bringing it to my lips as I always did with women I met in public. That was perhaps the only public display of affection I engaged in, all because Sydney advised me to do so, as I refused to kiss women on the cheek even after Anna left me.

"It's an honor, Mr. President." Leona then turned to shake Zachary's hand, who was next to me.

He was lucky to be married and not have to greet with kisses. He wasn't the type to enjoy congratulating with kisses. But apparently, doing so made female voters feel more affectionate, which was good for a future candidacy.

The orchestra that was playing would accompany Leona in her performance. Her voice was impeccably beautiful. I bade farewell to the stage, opening the dance floor, without even having a chance to descend the steps from the stage because my cousin immediately made a gesture with his head for me to follow, wanting to discuss the matter I had started.

CHAPTER TWENTY-EIGHT

Hazel

I didn't approach my family again; I stayed by the side of the hall, in a more secluded corner, watching the president speak into the microphone. What was the need to kiss that woman's hand? *Damn it!*

I was jealous. Jealous of a kiss on the hand, something I knew he did with every woman he met, but now it was different. I knew those lips had touched mine, so it felt like they belonged to me alone.

"Miss." I turned my face to see a waiter bringing more champagne glasses. He left the empty one there, and I took another full one, the third one. I should slow down, but the problem was that I was a bit out of control.

I was alone again. Letting out a long sigh, I turned knowing I needed to go back to the table with my sister; after all, they would notice my absence.

"Wait," the voice behind me made me turn and lift my face.

I knew it was him, the only one with that pleasant tone to hear.

"How did you find me?" I said, raising an eyebrow.

"You're not in such a hidden place." He shrugged subtly, without even realizing clearly what he was doing.

"Yeah." I brought the glass to my lips, taking just a sip, soon seeing the glass being taken from my fingers. — *Hey!*

"Every time I find you, you have a glass in your hand; you're going to end up getting drunk." He extended his hand, placing the glass on a piece of furniture nearby.

"What does it matter?" I retorted.

"I bet you don't want to cause any trouble with your family."

"Always being the perfect gentleman." I rolled my eyes. "You can let go of my arm now, I got your message, no more champagne."

"We haven't talked yet. I want you to forgive me for not sending any messages during the week. I'm not good at this kind of thing anymore." He twisted his lip into a half-smile.

"Thing?" I tried to hold back a smile.

"Yeah, what we're having," Christopher didn't know how to describe or label what we had.

"What are we having, Mr. President?" I crossed my arms, teasing.

"I don't know..."

"I don't think we need to label it." I shook my head subtly.

"So you're apologizing then?" I gasped when Christopher grabbed my arms, holding onto one of my wrists. He knew where to go, confidently walking down a corridor, soon stopping in front of a door.

He turned the doorknob, opening it. Without waiting for me to say anything, he brought me inside, pushing me against the door and keeping it closed.

Roughly, he squeezed both sides of my face, as our eyes met and his lips descended abruptly onto mine, touching them with an impact that even produced a slight noise.

Locking our lips, our tongues touched, the friction causing our teeth to clash. I raised my hand and ran it through his hair, feeling its softness.

Christopher was big, his sculpted body; everything about that man fascinated me.

It was almost impossible to stop; there was no way to let go. The kiss became slow, tender, his tongue moving slowly over mine, and as I tilted my head, a sigh escaped my lips.

His fingers found the side slit of my dress, moving his hand along there, and I felt how he gripped my thigh with strength, his large fingers almost covering it completely.

"Chris..." his name came out as a moan from my mouth.

He didn't care about my moan, sliding one hand down to my butt, squeezing it and moving his lips to my neck, as he raised the other hand, pulling my hair into a ponytail.

"I don't want to stop," he growled while kissing my neck.

"Don't stop," I whispered.

"I can't let you go out looking all disheveled," he roared, taking a deep breath and removing his hand from my butt.

His touch there only confirmed that this man must be a machine in bed, holding me tightly, not afraid I would break like a fragile crystal.

"No." I shrugged my shoulders.

"I would never let anyone think you're the type of woman who clings in corners." A smile appeared on my lips.

"Mr. President, but I was clinging." I bit the corner of my lip, walking towards him.

Christopher raised his hand as if to place the strands of my hair in place.

"You're strange," I whispered, meeting his eyes.

"I like to take care of what I have beside me." He winked and then touched the corner of my lip, clearly wiping it clean.

I turned my head so I could touch his lip with my tongue, circling his finger.

"Little troublemaker," he whispered, and I smiled mischievously.

"You're too proper." I touched Christopher's waist.

"I brought something for you." He reached inside his jacket. "It wasn't meant to be a gift as an apology, but I think it will serve that purpose."

Christopher took out a small red box from his pocket, and when I opened it, it revealed a pair of small earrings.

"They match your eyes," he whispered, and I took them between my fingers. They were indeed very beautiful, small, with a blue gem in each of them.

"Christopher, this... this is beautiful," I murmured, enchanted by their beauty, "but I'm not sure if I should accept it."

"You definitely should accept it, Hazel. I saw them in the hotel store's display, and you immediately came to mind." He touched the side of my hair, tucking it behind my ear.

Carefully, Christopher removed the earring I was wearing and put on the ones he had bought.

"You look incredibly beautiful," he whispered, lowering his face and giving a peck on my lips.

"You're a true gentleman, Mr. President," I murmured, biting the corner of my lip.

"And you, my little troublemaker." He bit my lip, pulling it back.

The way he said "my" felt as if he could claim me right then and there.

"Do we really need to leave here? Can we leave and go straight to somewhere we can be alone?" I declared, my voice breathy.

"You mean we're leaving together tonight?" Christopher tightened his hold on my waist.

"I don't know, if I happen to get an invitation." I gave a mischievous half-smile.

"I'll enlist the help of my assistant." Christopher let out a long sigh. "We need to leave, keep an eye on your phone, I'll send messages on it..."

"Now you're going to send them?" I teased him.

"I'll always send them." He winked, and I melted inside.

CHAPTER TWENTY-NINE

Hazel

Since we returned to the table, my brother-in-law hadn't taken his eyes off me. It was as if he knew everything, even though we hadn't arrived together. I had shown up well before Christopher, so there was no way he could suspect anything based on that delay.

Some appetizers were served, at least this way I could eat a bit and not get drunk on champagne.

Christopher didn't stay in one place; he was always with groups of politicians, and when he wasn't with one, he appeared in another.

Zachary, on the other hand, stayed closer to his wife, but whenever he needed to go talk to someone, my sister went with him.

"Why does your cousin keep moving around while you stay put, Zach?" I asked, stopping beside my brother-in-law.

"Simple, he's the one in demand, not me." He shrugged while caressing his wife's shoulder.

"And you still intend to run for president knowing how hectic it is, wanting to try for a third child," I mocked.

"First, let's focus on Chris; he'll want to run again. I have time for a third child and still enjoy them a bit." He shrugged.

My sister looked up, affectionately at her husband.

"We'll all be cheering you on up there, dear," I made a face at her words.

"You two make me nauseous," I grumbled, and at that moment, the president stopped beside us.

"Don't you think a wife should stand by her husband, proudly following his steps?" Christopher asked. Our conversations always started like this, with one poking at the other.

"That's not the issue. I'm not against a couple being proud of each other; after all, I know my brother-in-law is proud of Sav, and if he's not, I still have my gun under the seat of my pickup." I squinted my eyes at Zachary, who managed to stifle a laugh. "But you two are so clingy, you know those people who were born to be attached to each other? That's you."

I pointed at the couple, letting out a restrained laugh to avoid drawing attention.

"And that's not a good thing?" Zach teased amid his question.

"No, I don't think I could ever live with someone who's a hundred percent like me. There needs to be that spark of conflict." I shrugged, expressing my thoughts.

"That's why you're still single," Zachary mocked again.

"Darling, I have my whole life ahead of me; I'm not desperately chasing after a man." I winked.

"I pity the man who decides to be with you," my brother-in-law was a master at mockery.

"I don't. He'll be a very lucky man," I retorted playfully.

"I think the man who ends up with Hazel will need to be quite resilient, since she's a woman full of opinions," Natalie, who was present, also joined the conversation.

"Since when did my love life become a topic here?" I asked, narrowing my eyes.

"Dear, you're beautiful, wonderful, and strong. I would have loved to be your mother-in-law, but my son is closed off to new relationships." Natalie rolled her eyes, looking at Christopher.

"That's only going to happen by a miracle," I mocked as I always did, so no one would suspect anything.

"I still believe in miracles." The president's mother had a hopeful look.

"I'm going to talk to Governor Parker," Christopher clearly wanted to escape that embarrassing conversation and moved away.

"One has only one child, and he comes with a flaw," Natalie complained as soon as the president left.

"We can't have everything, dear. You already have a presidential son to be proud of." Grace, Zachary's mother, raised her hand to touch Natalie's.

The ladies were sitting next to each other while their husbands conversed with other men in another group.

"You have both: a beautiful daughter-in-law, grandchildren, and a son who wants to be president. What greater pride could there be?" Natalie pointed to Sav but looked at Grace.

"But Christopher has been married before; it's necessary to respect his decision." Grace defended her nephew.

"Yes, but he deserves to experience a new love. I remember well how attentive he was with Anna. It's not fair for a good man like Chris to die alone." The mother shrugged her shoulders.

All I heard was the name of the late wife and how attentive he had been with her. Would I ever have all that? Was it too wrong to compare myself to a woman who wasn't even alive anymore?

"Everyone talks about this, but I never asked, what was he like as a husband?" My sister joined the conversation.

This should have been the moment for me to step away, but my jealous side kept me there to torment myself.

"Chris was a good husband; they complemented each other in every way, so much alike that they seemed to be that type of couple who were made for each other. Anna was loving; she liked our family, and we all liked her. Most importantly, she supported Christopher, standing by him through everything that came their way. My son was madly in love with her. They were married and expecting their first child, but this fact is not mentioned by anyone; only we in the family know. Anna hadn't publicly announced the pregnancy; it was an early stage. They were going to wait until she completed three months, but my daughter-in-law was passionate about that motorcycle, the same one that took her life." Natalie let out a sigh of lament.

"Oh, I didn't know she was pregnant." My sister showed surprise.

I hadn't known that either; he hadn't just lost his wife, but also a child. The family that was about to start was destroyed by a motorcycle accident.

"Chris, even though he's been in this eternal mourning, is a strong man. I don't know if I could live in a world where my wife isn't," Zachary spoke thoughtfully, bending down to give his wife a kiss on the top of her head.

"Or maybe life is showing him that it can give him a second chance to love," Natalie remained confident, as if she knew her son deserved much more than that solitude.

I turned my face, observing from a distance as Christopher talked with some politicians. A serious man who, looking at him like this, one could hardly imagine that he carried within him a pain capable of tearing anyone apart.

CHAPTER THIRTY

Hazel

"Dear, can we go?" Savannah asked Zachary. My sister was clearly exhausted, especially since she was often the one waking up in the middle of the night to nurse Alexis.

"Yes, let's go." Zachary ran his hand down his wife's back, pulling her close.

At that moment, Christopher approached. Most people had already left, even Scarlett had gone with her parents. She seemed off, which made me wonder if she had spoken to Malcolm and he said something she didn't like. I would need to call Scar and ask if they had talked.

"Cousin, we're leaving," Zachary said to Christopher.

"Alright," he nodded.

"Hazel, we'll go in the front car, and you can go in the one that will come right after." I just nodded, as the president hadn't sent me any message, which was a clear sign that we wouldn't be seeing each other.

"Why is she going in another car if she could come with us?" my sister immediately asked, making a face at her husband.

"Can't a husband have some alone time with his wife? At home, time is short." He winked at Sav.

"Oh, I definitely don't want to be a third wheel." I made a face at the couple.

Savannah didn't argue against Zachary's request because they were always with their two daughters and didn't get much time alone.

After saying goodbye, they went ahead, and I was left alone. They asked me to wait ten minutes, as my car would soon be available to take me to my sister's house. I would spend the night there and leave the next day.

I hadn't realized that Christopher was still beside me until he made a movement and I looked at him.

"Come with me?" I was puzzled by that request.

"Huh?" I made a face.

"Yes, you heard me right. Come with me, we're going to my house," he whispered so that no one could hear us.

"Your house, the White House?" It was impossible not to widen my eyes.

"As far as I know, that's where I live." Christopher gave a small smile.

"Can I go in?" I still hadn't processed it.

"Of course you can, you're my guest." He seemed to be holding back a laugh.

"Don't laugh at me." I crossed my arms.

"Alright, if you can go now, your car is waiting for you. Everything has been prepared for your arrival there; I'll follow soon after." I felt his fingers delicately holding mine in a way that was barely noticeable.

"Zachary, does he know?" I squinted my eyes.

"I might have let it slip." Christopher frowned.

"Oh, my sister will kill me when she finds out that her husband knew first." I sighed loudly. "And they say women are the gossips."

I grumbled, turning around since we couldn't even say goodbye. Spending that night in Christopher's presence, even if from a distance, made me realize that the man never stopped, always giving attention to someone different.

In his gaze, it was clear he loved all of it, the kind of man who was born to lead a country.

I left the luxurious event; a car was already waiting for me, and as if they knew me, the door was opened as soon as I arrived.

"Miss Bellingham." The driver bowed his head in a greeting.

I just nodded with a smile and sat down alone in the back seat. The same man who opened the door for me got behind the wheel and started the car.

I was quite anxious, afraid of what my stay at Christopher's house might bring. I wasn't the type to feel fear; I was more practical. I knew all my partners, and they weren't like the president, so I didn't have any expectations.

But with Christopher, it was different. He had that magnetism; our bodies always seemed to connect, as if all our differences guided us.

I focused my attention on the road, observing everything around me as the car passed through the streets. The countless lights were what drew my attention; we were arriving at the White House.

The lawn was an incredibly beautiful shade of green, clearly visible thanks to the numerous lights illuminating it.

We stopped in front of the gate. Before it was opened, a flashlight was shone on the driver's face as if they were identifying him.

It didn't take more than a minute for the gates to open. I felt like a little child, looking at everything around me. I should have behaved like a woman of class, but all I wanted to do was run around that house.

For now, I would restrain myself.

Slowing down, we stopped in front of the facade. Out of nowhere, someone appeared to open the door for me, and I took the hand that was extended to me.

As soon as I set foot on the ground, my hands fell to my sides.

"Miss, please follow me," the same man who opened my door requested.

I didn't question it; I just followed. Climbing the small flight of stairs, I passed through the porch, and the doors were opened by two women as we approached.

"Welcome, Miss," they said in unison, nodding their heads in greeting.

"Would you like something to eat, Miss?" the man who was accompanying me asked.

"Oh, no," I murmured, admiring the perfect entrance hall.

What were the chances of running off and getting lost in that enormous house? The same house I had only seen in photos and had briefly visited with my sister. Now it was different; I was a direct guest of the president.

"I'll show you to your room." I just nodded, as if my voice had been taken from me.

How did Christopher manage to live alone in that vast mansion and not feel lonely? It must be why he was so bitter. With so many rooms where one could easily get lost, and seeing staff who didn't seem very comfortable talking to the president of the country.

I figured even I would be uncomfortable if my boss were the president of the country.

I held onto the railing, which was a golden hue, reflecting even me.

We continued down a hallway, lined with portraits of all the presidents the country had ever had. I could swear there must be the same portraits elsewhere in the house, as it was a monstrous size.

I stopped in front of the last portrait, displayed there, and it was him. The most handsome man I had ever seen. The current president, Christopher Fitzgerald, with the year of his candidacy and his age.

Certainly, God must have his favorites. He was handsome, incredibly intelligent, and had been celibate for twelve years, a fact that left me curious and simultaneously anxious.

"Do you like what you're seeing?" The whisper in my ear made every hair on my body stand on end.

I turned my face and saw him there, the same man from the portrait: Christopher Fitzgerald.

CHAPTER THIRTY-ONE

Christopher

I intertwined my hand with hers. The man who had been accompanying Hazel had already stepped away; now it was just the two of us. Everyone at the White House signed a confidentiality agreement to keep what happened inside confidential.

"You look incredibly delicious in that portrait." Hazel turned and, with her free hand, touched my neck.

"Delicious isn't a word often used to describe me." I gave a brief smile.

I pulled her by her slender waist, her body pressing against mine. Hazel was so small she could fit perfectly in my arms.

"It's because you don't have the habit of dating women." She bit the corner of her lip without taking her eyes off mine.

"It's not something I miss, with one exception." I lowered my face, gently touching her lips.

"What exception?" Her mouth slightly parted, letting out a sigh.

"You, my only exception." I nipped at her lip.

"Is that good?"

"Absolutely, yes. I'm addicted to you, like I haven't been in a long time, I barely remember what addiction was like," I whispered, pushing her against the wall.

"Christopher." She sighed, and with practicality, I lifted her in my arms.

Hazel easily spread her legs due to the slit in the side of her dress, allowing her to wrap around my waist.

"I need to take you to my room..."

"Please, President, don't ask, just take me, take me to your room" her voice was muffled by the intense kiss I demanded from her lips.

The presidential suite was just next door, and without stopping the kiss as I walked down the corridor, I stopped in front of my room, pushing the door open with my body and turned on the light with one hand, which I removed from her body, while guiding Hazel to the center of my bed.

Her fingers never left my neck, and I felt her nails scratching delightfully at my skin.

I pinched her lower lip between my teeth, pulling at it, and Hazel let out a husky moan. The room suddenly felt stuffy, or perhaps it was the heat emanating from every part of my body. I subtly pulled back as my body covered hers.

"Christopher" her voice came out in a hoarse moan.

"Say it, little one" I whispered, focusing on her swollen and reddened lips from our kiss.

It was incredibly addictive, having that image left me a madman, Hazel was like a drug, the closer I got, savoring her little by little, the more I became a complete addict.

"Don't stop" she whispered as she lifted her hand and touched the corner of my arm.

"That's not an option." I moved away, standing and removing my jacket, throwing it on the floor as I easily took off my tie.

Hazel sat on the bed. Her fingers touched the sheet as she looked at me with lust while opening each button of my shirt. I left it on the floor along with the rest of my clothes and stepped out of my shoes.

Kneeling on the bed, I felt her delicate fingers touch my waist, as they moved up to the center of my chest, and our eyes met.

"It's such a tremendous cruelty for someone to be as beautiful as you" she murmured, kissing my chest. "Tell me one of your flaws, President..."

"I'm controlling, and that can be a big flaw." I lowered my gaze, seeing her tongue leave a trail there.

"A big flaw." I gasped when the little one bit my chest. "You have firm skin, it's hard to bite."

She teased, moving on the bed, removing and, without looking, throwing her shoe.

"Are you sure about that?" She had that sparkle in her eyes, as if she wanted it more than anything, but was apprehensive about what my decision might be.

"Yes, I'm sure" I spoke with conviction, there was no doubt. She was the one, my chosen one.

The only one who challenged me. It was as if there was never any sameness. Hazel was a force of nature, she didn't conform to what I wanted to hear, always sincere, in a way no one else could be.

In the world I lived in, people tended to be malleable and often deceitful, trying to cater to my desires, or even false. And that was something I could not tolerate.

"Christopher, do we need to set any boundaries?" she asked, and I frowned, not understanding the reason for her question.

"Boundaries of what kind?"

"I'm not some puritan virgin, but I've never been involved with another man, like in a relationship. I'm not one to get attached, I think it's simply because I've never had feelings. You've had that, and you've been alone for a long time. I want to know if what we're going to have is just sex? Because if it's only sex, it's better for me..."

"You only want me for sex?" I interrupted her abruptly.

"You're the president of our country and I'm just a dreamy girl from Arizona. What do you want from me? I'd never be on your level, so I'd rather be very aware if it's just sex. — She shrugged. — I'm not stupid,

I wasn't born to be a woman like Savannah, my sister adapts quickly to any environment. If we're going to have a relationship, I'd prefer no one knew about it, so we wouldn't give false hope to ourselves or anyone else."

The smile that appeared on her lips was clearly forced.

"Hazel." I sighed, holding the side of her dress. "Your social position was never a factor I considered. To be honest, I find you beautiful, amazing, with a strong opinion. Few women have the wisdom to sustain a conversation with any man in politics. Your arguments always annoyed me, which is due to the fascination I didn't want to admit I had."

I held the fabric of her dress, slowly pulling it up and over her head. Hazel was a woman who understood politics, and every time I saw her talking with a member of parliament, it was clear she knew what she was talking about, her words were not empty or uninformed.

"I thought you didn't like intrusive people." She placed her hands over her breasts, covering them.

"Actually, I don't, but in your case, it's a delightful exception." I focused my attention on the woman kneeling.

Her delicate lace panties covered her small intimacy while her soft hands with painted pink nails covered her breasts.

Hazel was beautiful, and my eyes were addicted to watching her.

CHAPTER THIRTY-TWO

Hazel

I bit the corner of my lip as the president lowered himself, and gently, holding my wrists, removed my hands from covering my breasts. He pushed my body onto the bed, raising my arms above my head.

He lowered his gaze, fixed it on my face, and as our eyes met in that intense connection, he slowly continued to slide his gaze, stopping over my breasts.

I believed that this was the first time he was doing something without asking for permission. He raised his hands, glided his fingers over my breasts, as if they were tiny ants leaving tiny traces of delicious shocks on my skin.

Unexpectedly, he squeezed them hard, and a sudden, hoarse moan escaped my mouth.

"Delicious," he growled, lowering himself over me as he brought his mouth closer to my breasts, and I felt the exact moment his tongue circled my nipple. "Just as I expected, so smooth..."

His words died when he took my breast into his mouth and sucked on my nipple. I moaned as he continued to slide his tongue without removing his mouth, as if he were sucking and licking it.

I touched his hair, running my fingers through Christopher's head, tilting my head back, while one of his hands squeezed my breasts and the other moved down my waist.

I bit my lips hard as the president switched to the other breast, now taking it into his mouth. He bit, licked, sucked, and squeezed with intensity, as if he couldn't realize the extent of his strength.

It wasn't bad, quite the opposite. It was the first time someone took me like that. It wasn't gentle, and I might even thank him for that.

He began to lower his face, leaving bites and licks along my stomach. His two hands continued to squeeze my breasts, pinching the tip of my nipple as if he knew it would make me moan more.

His face rested in the center of my pleasure. I lifted my face as our eyes met, and Christopher lowered his hands, still dragging his fingers across my stomach.

Holding both sides of my panties, he lowered them down my legs, but instead of throwing them on the floor, he placed them on the side of the bed, on the piece of furniture there.

Without saying a word, he fixed his gaze on the center of my pleasure, just as he had done with my breasts, analyzing it, and holding my knees, pushed them apart, as I automatically bent them, giving him full visibility of my pussy.

I wasn't usually a shy person, but with Christopher looking at me that way, it was like feeling my face catch fire.

"Perfect..." he whispered, placing a knee on the bed.

Without asking for permission, he touched me again, as if his fingers were discovering a new toy. I felt his thumb pass over the center of my pussy, spreading my vaginal lips.

It was incredible how that man worshipped me. Christopher was much more than just a handsome man; he knew how to look, how to worship, and above all, dominate a woman just with his gaze.

"You know, Hazel," he murmured, raising his intense blue eyes toward me. "I didn't know I needed sex so much until I had you this way in my bed."

"President, you can become addicted to just me." I bit the corner of my lip, rolling my eyes as he inserted just one finger into my pussy.

"So tight... *hot*," he whispered as his finger moved in and out of my intimacy.

"Chris," I moaned with one of his thumbs caressing my folds while the other took me.

"Call me that, drop the 'sir' from your speech..."

"I like how I can provoke you with the simple word *sir*, it sounds so sexy." My slightly open mouth let out soft sighs.

"I'm starting to think that a relationship between incompatible people might become my new sin," Christopher knew how to speak with a husky voice, driving me to delirium just with the hand that touched me.

"Let me be your sin, president, please end this anguish that consumes us," I pleaded.

"No need to ask, you already are." The president removed his fingers from my pussy.

Straightening his body, he opened the drawer and took out a condom.

"Wait, that hasn't been in there for twelve years, has it?" A forced laugh escaped my lips.

"No, of course not, it's been there for about a week..."

"A week?" I squinted my eyes.

"The exact time since I invited you to come to my house, not that I planned on having sex, but I needed to be prepared in case the occasion arose. I couldn't be unprepared."

"Yes, you are a very prepared man." I looked down at his bare chest, which was large with defined muscle marks. I could have fun with that piece of bad news for a lifetime.

Christopher placed the condom on the bed and unbuttoned his pants, sliding down the fabric, leaving him in just that black boxer brief. I bit the corner of my lip, unable to take my eyes off those toned legs, which were even bigger than mine, though that wasn't hard to achieve.

"Do you know if there's popcorn for watching this show?" I teased as he looked up at me.

Christopher pulled down his underwear. He had no shame; for a man who had spent many years without a partner, he wasn't shy, and with that body, how could he be?

His penis sprang out as the fabric fell, and it was huge, oh God! The biggest member I had ever seen. I wasn't a woman who had seen many, but I knew enough to understand that this one was enormous, large, with a thick girth, and veins marked it, leaving the tip with a slight sheen.

"Christopher," I whispered as he took the condom. "You know that after you, no other man will have the chance to excite me."

The mention of another man made him glance quickly at me.

"Another man? Who said you'll need another man?" The condom covered Christopher's entire penis.

"What do you mean by that?" I bit the tip of my finger.

"That if it depends on me, you'll only have one man in your life." His body came over mine, our eyes locked on each other. "That someone will be *me*!"

CHAPTER THIRTY-THREE

Christopher

My body pressed against hers. Hazel was small; even with her legs wrapped around my waist, she couldn't fully clasp them around my back.

Unable to contain myself, my penis quickly made contact with the small spot of her pussy and pressed against it. I began taking her, closing my eyes in response to the primitive grunt that escaped my mouth.

It was like being choked, in a good way.

"Chris..." Hazel moaned, and our eyes met. "Don't hold back, give me all of you."

"Yes," I grunted with an abrupt thrust.

She was tight; my penis didn't fill her completely. I withdrew and re-entered, thrusting again.

I slid my hand down her waist, touched her shoulder, and then moved to her neck, spreading my fingers in her hair, intertwining them and pulling with a little force.

"Tell me if anything bothers you," I growled, keeping my eyes locked on hers.

"Nothing can bother me." Hazel's nails scratched my shoulder.

It was like losing my virginity a second time. The woman beneath me was beautiful, perfect in every way.

"I won't be able to last much longer this first time; I feel like an adolescent at the peak of puberty," I whispered with my other hand gripping her breasts and pinching her pointed nipples.

"So you couldn't control yourself when you were an adolescent?" She gave me a mischievous smile.

"Let's just say it was good to carry the Fitzgerald surname." I lowered my face, biting her lip.

"So you weren't always the perfect gentleman?" Hazel was even more beautiful when she teased.

"I had my bad boy phase," I murmured, thrusting harder.

"I'd say I'd love to meet you in that phase, but I forget that you hadn't even outgrown diapers then." A delightful laugh escaped her lips.

"No, you wouldn't want to." I removed my hand from her hair, touching Hazel's neck.

"Tell me what you did to get a woman in your bed?" I said nothing, only changed the way I looked at her.

I didn't divert my gaze; I just marked every feature of her, marking her as mine, wanting her to feel unique with just my look. There was no need to talk when all I needed was to dominate her, to excite her.

"Is this what you did?" I winked, making it clear that it was. "Oh God, if she were in panties, I'd believe she must be completely wet at that moment."

Hazel didn't say anything more; our bodies collided, my penis thrusting into her forcefully. I needed her, needed her with all my strength. Hazel was even more beautiful when she was sweaty, with her lips slightly parted and moans escaping.

I tightened my grip on her neck slightly. Her walls tightened around my penis, but apparently, I wasn't the only one giving in easily.

I continued thrusting harder, in and out strongly, until I felt the liquid burst forth, relieving me. It was like releasing years of celibacy from within me as I gave myself to that little goddess of love.

I let my body fall on top of hers, our sweaty chests and heavy breathing filling the room.

I knew Hazel would soon complain about my weight, so I got off her, stood up, and removed the condom, tossing it in the suite's trash can.

I returned to the room where Hazel was sitting, watching me. She bit the corner of her lip. Unashamedly, she let her eyes travel down my body as I approached, sat on the bed, and without saying a word, she swung a leg on either side of my waist, straddling me and sitting on my lap.

"You know, Chris." Her fingers touched my shoulder. "You live up to your reputation."

I smiled wickedly as Hazel slid her fingers down my chest. How could I have lived so many days since meeting this daring woman without this, without the sensation of her touches, her body on mine, our intimacy? It was as if my body was preparing, making it clear that we would be dominated by a woman.

"Live up to my reputation?" I squinted my eyes.

"Yeah, they say all Fitzgeralds are naturally good in bed." She let out a hearty laugh.

"Oh, I don't want to know about the prowess of my cousins, and I'm wary that you do." I curled my lip.

"How could I not know? My sister is married to one, my friend is married to another. You know, we share information, not me, of course, I don't have many good stories." Knowing this triggered my possessive side.

"I like it even less." I grumbled, feeling her rub her pussy against my semi-erect penis.

"Christopher Fitzgerald, I'm not yours to be jealous of." She tilted her head back, her long blonde waves brushing against my leg.

"Not yet." She looked up.

I gripped the base of my cock, wanting her to ride it.

"Is it always like this? Taking everything for yourself?" Hazel didn't question the fact that I wanted her to ride me.

"Not everything, only what I most desire to have by my side," I whispered with a growl as she filled me, sitting on my cock.

Hazel bit her lip, her pointed breasts brushing against my chest.

"Do you want me, Christopher Fitzgerald?" It was clear from her tone that she was mocking, teasing, but my response was more serious than she expected.

"Yes, my daring one, I'm not at an age to play around. I'm not the type to take curves. When I want something, I pursue it with all my conviction." I slid my hand down her waist, squeezing both sides of her ass and pushing her forcefully closer to my cock.

"Talking like that." Hazel kept grinding on my penis. "I might even pretend to believe it..."

How could she believe I was lying? Was it my social position? My political career? Our age difference? If it were those things, they would never matter to me. Just the fact that she had touched my heart, made me so vulnerable—something no one had managed to do for many years—already made her special.

Hazel wrapped her arms around my neck, but I didn't let go of her ass, letting her grind on my cock, enjoying her lips in a slow, wet kiss, with my tongue intertwined with hers in a delicious melody.

"I need more, let me take you from behind," it was strange to speak like that again; after all, I was always so proper, but if there was something I couldn't be proper about, it was there, in bed, with her.

"Yes, my president, fuck me." She pulled away, licking around her lip. Damn it! She would drive me mad.

Without hesitation, Hazel knew she was small, so she got on all fours on the bed, sticking her ass up, her head on the mattress, perfectly positioned for my cock to take her.

I brushed my penis against her entrance, holding both sides of her ass, and started thrusting with force. From the side of her face, which was turned on the bed, I could see her biting her lip as she gripped the sheets.

The friction of my pelvis slamming against her ass echoed in the room. Our sighs, Hazel's loud moans, etched into my memory.

"Hazel... my little daring one," I grunted, giving her ass a slap that turned red from my grip.

"Yes, my president, hit me..." she begged, and I gave her what she wanted, delivering another slap to the other side of her ass.

I grabbed her hair, pulling it into a ponytail and yanked her face back.

"Tell me, who's the only one capable of dominating you like this?" I roared in my primitive way.

"You, you, my president." Her eyes met mine, and even sweaty, with her makeup slightly smudged, nothing made her less beautiful.

I continued penetrating her forcefully, going all the way in, claiming every part of her.

I could easily become a sexual maniac if I had that little sex kitten by my side.

Hazel was sweet and spicy in the perfect measure. And I, a forty-year-old man, was crazy about her.

The little one came first, and when I felt her convulse, with one last thrust, I came deep inside her, only realizing at that moment that we were without a condom.

Damn, how did I not notice that?

CHAPTER THIRTY-FOUR

Hazel

I sat on the bed and brought my finger to my mouth as Christopher left the suite right after me.

We took a shower together, and I have to admit I was apprehensive since I had never showered with a man before. Christopher was gentle, washing every part of my body. He couldn't keep his hands off me, which was somehow advantageous for me because I got to wash the president.

His back was broad; everything about him was big, unlike me.

I could even feel my intimacy throbbing after the sex we had, and during the shower, I realized we should take a break; I wasn't used to so much sex.

Christopher was wearing only sweatpants, barefoot, and stopped in front of me.

"I asked Sydney to leave something for you to wear." He went towards the door.

I watched him return with a paper bag bearing the Louis Vuitton name on it.

"You could wear my dress," I said, grabbing the bag.

"Not a chance." I looked inside the bag, which was actually better because I didn't want to go out in the evening gown.

The fact that it was Louis Vuitton didn't impress me; my sister had a lot of clothes from that brand, as if the Fitzgeralds didn't know what a thrift store was.

I made a face as I got up, which caught Christopher's attention, and he gave me a concerned look.

"Is something wrong?" he asked immediately.

"I don't think I'm used to having sex so many times in a row, and with a member like..." I made a gesture with my hand indicating a large size, making him burst into a loud laugh at the way I chose to speak.

"Maybe I went in too eager, wanting to make up for all my time in one night." Christopher sat on the bed.

I took the clothes out of the bag, noticing there were jeans, a jacket, and even a pair of flats.

"It's too much, Christopher." I looked up at him. "I didn't mind wearing my heels."

"Hazel, just accept it." His tone had that possessive timbre.

I made a face, rolling my eyes.

"You know I'm not a child, right?" I took the towel off my hair. I needed to wash it since Christopher ended up getting it wet during our sex.

"Far from it, you're a beautiful woman."

"Then don't treat me like one, telling me what I need to do. We just had sex, and you're already saying 'just accept it.' Chris, you need to understand that I know how much money you have; you don't need to win me over with it." I touched his shoulder, standing between his legs. "If I'm with you, it's for who you are..."

"I'd never think that. I know the family you come from." He untied my robe, opening it and bringing his mouth to my belly, smelling it. "You just need to understand that I love taking care of what's mine. I'm the type who loves to pamper."

I touched his hair, running my hands down his broad back, and we stayed like that for long seconds. Words weren't necessary; our bodies just connected.

"Hazel, you need to take one of those pills tomorrow; we can't risk having a child from a relationship that's not even a marriage," he asked, and I looked down.

"I'll buy them; I don't want to be a mother for now." I pouted.

"For now?" He furrowed his brow.

"My dream is to be a mother, to wake up in the middle of the night to that little cry. Fun baths, first steps, everything." I could swear my eyes sparkled when I shared that.

"I'm sure you'll be a great mother." He gave a brief, forced smile.

"Chris, I know; your mother told me about... about... the pregnancy." I pouted.

His body tensed; I didn't think I had made the wrong decision. Christopher slowly let go of my waist.

"I'm sorry; I shouldn't have brought it up." I stepped back, grabbing the bag and seeing the lingerie inside, picking it up, it was lace, delicate.

"No, it's not you. I just don't like talking about it. I was supposed to have a twelve-year-old child, a wife, a family, possibly more children, or not, because Anna always said she wanted only one child, unlike me, who didn't want just one. I'm an only child and I know how lonely a life without siblings can be." His eyes didn't stray from mine.

"I'm sure you would be an amazing father." I smiled, putting on the lingerie.

"I've had everything taken from me; twelve years have passed, I've moved on." I frowned, skeptical about what he said. "I'm serious, I wouldn't be talking openly about it if it weren't a resolved matter."

I fastened the bra on my back. Our eyes met again.

"It's strange, you've lived through all of this, you've fallen in love, loved, married, experienced everything intensely..." I picked up the jeans with my fingers, biting the tip of my lip, unsure if I should touch on this topic.

"Yes, and that's why I wasn't thinking about starting over," Christopher picked up the shirt, holding it out to me as I finished putting on the jeans. "Until everything started to change between us. It wasn't something that happened overnight, and when that kiss almost happened, I decided it was time to end my mourning."

"So you admit you were in mourning?"

"Yes, I couldn't just lie down with another woman. I didn't want a carnal exchange; if it had to happen, it would be with the woman I was sure was right for me." I moved closer to him as I got dressed.

"You mean I'm the right one?" I sat back down on his lap.

"For many years, I hadn't been so excited just waking up and imagining you by my side. Your daring ways won me over, which is strange since Anna was very much in line with my tastes, opinions, and everything else, like love at first sight. And with you, it's different; we've been building everything, block by block. But it's always been you; I just didn't want to admit that the most daring woman was taking over my thoughts." Christopher held my waist. "You know, with you everything is different. It's like I'm experiencing everything anew."

I brought my lips close to his, a lingering peck turned into a slow kiss.

"You really can't stay here with me?" he whispered in the midst of the kiss.

"Did you forget that for now it's still a secret? I need to go to Zachary's house because with any luck, my sister will already be asleep and I can curl up in Sadie's room." I smiled, tilting my head back as his lips touched my neck.

"Okay, but will you stay here with me tomorrow?"

"Aren't we moving too fast?" I furrowed my brow.

"I want to be able to sleep and wake up next to you. Will you sleep with me, my little daring one?" he asked, touching the corner of my cheek.

"How can I say no to that whole body?"

"Oh, now I'm just a body?" he teased maliciously.

"Look, that doesn't make you any less of a man, not even the president of the country." Christopher got up from the bed, carrying me in his arms.

"I'll take you to the exit, leaving my sweet girl at your carriage..."

"I could easily become spoiled," I hugged him around the shoulder.

CHAPTER THIRTY-FIVE

Hazel

"Godmother" the child's voice filled my ears, and I opened one eye to see the little girl with messy hair beside me. "How come I didn't see you sleeping here?"

She was making one of those puzzled pouts.

"When I arrived, the little girl was already asleep." I sat up in bed, pushing my hair back.

"I see." In a funny way, my goddaughter shook her head.

Sadie jumped off the bed and headed for the bedroom door, probably calling my sister. I dragged myself to the suite, washing my face and brushing my hair. I was still wearing the same clothes from when I left Christopher's house. I arrived late and didn't want to make noise, so I just ended up falling asleep from sheer exhaustion.

When I left the suite, my sister was already there. Savannah looked me up and down.

"New clothes?" She crossed her arms. "Don't try to make excuses. You took a long time to arrive yesterday, and now you're wearing new clothes that look like they're from Louis Vuitton."

Savannah was sharp at connecting the dots; she wanted me to tell the truth and would notice if I lied.

"Well, I was with someone." I bit the corner of my lip.

"Do I know him?" She broke into a wide smile.

"Yes" my niece interrupted us at that moment, asking her mother for help with which outfit she should wear.

"Breakfast is served, you should eat, sister." Savannah winked, making it clear that she wanted to know more about the guy I was seeing, which was a clear sign that Zachary hadn't said anything.

I nodded and turned to leave the room, walking down the hallway. I could hear Zachary's voice talking to someone, and I recognized that tone.

Was Christopher there? I quickened my pace, approaching the dining room where breakfast was laid out, while slowing down and trying to overhear their conversation:

"Cousin, she's Savannah's sister; any fight between you two, I'll side with her. After all, my wife would never leave her sister in the lurch" the way Zachary spoke made me feel terrible for having omitted that information from my sister.

"There won't be any fights" Christopher seemed as impatient as ever.

"You two are always arguing, which makes me wonder how the hell you ended up in the same bed, especially since you were living in that years-long mourning." I put my finger to my mouth, curious to hear his answer.

"There's no explanation; I just know it's her" that was so Christopher.

I hadn't stopped to think about how he spoke with all those words that I belonged to him. How crazy could all of this be?

I felt like things were moving too fast. We'd only had one night of sex, and even before that, he was already saying I was his.

Tired of listening through the door, I cleared my throat and entered the breakfast room.

"Good morning" I said, but all I felt were my cheeks heating up when I met Christopher's gaze.

He looked incredibly handsome that morning. He wasn't wearing his usual suit but a polo shirt neatly folded at the neck.

"Hello, sister-in-law" Zach had a teasing tone in his voice.

"Did you sleep well, Hazel?" Christopher gave me one of his lovely smiles.

"If you're quick, you can greet each other with a kiss." Zachary rolled his eyes.

I just smiled and without questioning, practically ran to the president, bending down and giving him a lingering peck on the lips.

"You're still going to spend the night with me, aren't you?" He touched the corner of my cheek with his thumb.

"What do I get in return?" I teased mischievously.

"We can talk about that." I slowly moved away from him.

"Look, I don't like any of this. Savannah needs to know; she'll be very upset if she finds out from someone else" Zachary chided, but just then, my sister walked into the room.

Her eyes went straight to Christopher and then to me. She had clearly heard what her husband had said.

"What are you hiding from me?" Savannah crossed her arms.

"Sister, I was going to tell you." I gave a forced smile.

"Even Zachary knew before I did? I thought we were best friends" Savannah was upset. "Were you with Christopher last night?"

"Yes" I didn't lie.

"Does anyone else know besides Zachary?" I bit the corner of my lip, considering whether to mention that Scarlett also knew.

"Sweetheart, I don't think it's anything serious. They just didn't want to talk about it because they weren't sure if it would work out" my brother-in-law tried to defuse the situation.

"No, the issue is that I thought we were best friends. I've always told you everything, Hazel." My sister's eyes even filled with tears.

Savannah turned away. I wanted to go after her, but Zachary stood up from his chair first.

"Let it go, Hazel, I'll talk to her first. Your sister is upset; we know how sentimental she is. I'll calm her down first, and I'm sure she'll come back smiling." He winked and walked away from me.

I looked back at Christopher, who was still sitting there.

"I didn't want her to find out this way. Savannah has always been my best friend as well as my sister. I've never hidden anything from her, and now I feel terrible" I murmured, watching him get up from the bed.

"I'm sure she'll understand." He placed his hand on my waist and pulled me close.

"I don't like upsetting my best person" I murmured, feeling his finger hold my chin.

"You two are the definition of the best sisterly relationship." Christopher's hand traveled down my back, landing on my butt.

"You know, I want that for my future children." I bit the corner of my lip mischievously. "Mr. President, you're very naughty today."

"Speaking of children reminds me of this." He reached into his pants pocket and pulled out a small box. "The pill to prevent pregnancy."

"Oh, thanks for not making me go to a pharmacy." I held the box in my fingers.

"You need to use some form of birth control; I want to be able to have sex without worry."

"I'm going to ask a question; don't take it the wrong way. But if you don't want to answer, I'll understand." He looked at me, waiting for me to start speaking. "Don't you want more children? I mean, considering you're forty..."

"Children aren't something that crosses my mind, not anymore. I had already planned not to have children, so I don't know how to answer that question. Everything was taken from me, and now you show up, like my light at the end of the tunnel." He lowered his gaze and gave me a lingering kiss.

I didn't bring up the topic again; after all, what could be said about something so delicate? I couldn't forget to take that pill, because I wasn't going to be the one to give Christopher a child.

CHAPTER THIRTY-SIX

Hazel

I grabbed my handbag and the keys to my truck. All my plans had gone awry; the night I had hoped to spend with Christopher didn't happen.

There was an urgent meeting; he needed to attend and stay on call with his assistant.

My sister eventually understood. I explained to her multiple times that I didn't want to upset her because, of all the people in the world, she was one of the last I wanted to see sad. Savannah had always been the more sentimental of the two of us, and seeing her hurt was like cutting a part of myself.

Christopher didn't even stay long at Zachary's house; as soon as he received the call, he left in a hurry. I wished I could have spent more time with him, but as it seemed, the president wasn't exactly the type to have free time. I needed to keep that in mind.

I got into my truck and started it up. For a Monday, the day had started well enough. It could have been better if I had received a message from him, or maybe I was just being emotional when it came to Christopher. All this talk of "mine" that he emphasized in his sentences started to mess with my head.

I stopped at a traffic light, grabbed my phone from the passenger seat, and quickly searched for Scarlett's name in my contacts. I made the call, putting it on speakerphone so I could drive and talk to her at the same time.

The phone rang three times before Scar answered.

"Hey, sweetie," I said, hearing her let out a weak laugh on the other end of the line.

"Hey, Hazel, I'm walking around campus. I didn't hear your call."

"Did I interrupt something?" I asked, noticing she was at college.

"No, I'm on a break between classes." She seemed to sigh.

"Did something happen between you and Malcolm? He said he was going to talk to you, and then I saw you looking even more down at the event." I wanted to know how Scar was doing.

"It happened just as I expected. He was a total jerk, Hazel, said it was better if we stayed apart, that the sex didn't mean anything. If I had any glimmer of hope, I should get that out of my mind since we wouldn't even exchange glances if it were up to him." Scar sniffled, making it clear she was crying. "I'm a disgrace to my family. They're all so confident, and here I am, crying over a man who snubbed me."

Luckily, at that moment, I was pulling up to the office and parked my truck away from all the other cars as I always did. Now I could give my friend my full attention.

"Scar, you're not a disgrace. He's the one losing a wonderful woman. Friend, in this way, it's better for you because now you can move on without setting any expectations, no matter how hard it is. Know that you can always call me, and if you want to get back at him, I'll be here too." I could hear her let out a weak laugh.

"No revenge, I think it's best to keep my distance. I know I'll get over my first romantic failure, even if it's with that handsome man, considering his photo is constantly in the media, not just because of politics but because he belongs to one of the most multibillion-dollar families."

"Look on the bright side. You're suffering over a handsome man; it could be worse; he could be an ugly loser." I laughed, hearing her do the same.

"Oh, heavens, I don't think I could ever be with one of those." Scar was restrained even in her laughter.

"So you just plan to stay away?" I asked, wanting to know about her plans.

"Yes, I'm just going to stay away from him. I can't humiliate myself more than I already have for a man who apparently slept with me as some petty revenge of his own, all because his sister married William. It hurts so much, knowing that Malcolm had me because he wanted to prove to himself that even though he was friends with my cousins, he still had one of them in his bed, as if getting even didn't hurt." Her voice became sad again. "But I'm fine; I'll be okay. I'll focus on my studies, graduate, and show that governor he means nothing in my life and pretend to myself that I never cried in front of him. I'm a failure, Hazel."

"Scar, if you want, I can arrange to come see you this weekend. Let's go out, have fun, and enjoy the weekend together. What do you think?" Scarlett had always been very solitary; her friends were carefully chosen, and when they didn't approach her just out of interest. Zoey was pregnant, so she wouldn't be able to meet Scarlett's needs at that moment, which is why I would be the friend she needed.

"But what about Chris, you two? Didn't anything happen?"

"Oh, yes, him..." I let out a weak laugh. "Your cousin is always busy; he won't even notice I went to see you."

"Thanks, Hazel, I do want your presence." I had to end the call and text her the time we'd meet.

I was almost late to start my shift, so I got out of the truck and ran towards the entrance.

I greeted some of the staff, placed my handbag under the desk, while turning on my computer and setting up my agenda next to me. Natalie's heels made me look up, as I recognized even her walking style.

But what surprised me most was seeing him next to her, her son, Christopher. He had his hands in his pockets, looking somewhat irritated, as if he hadn't slept much of the night.

"Hello, dear, good morning." Natalie was as helpful as ever.

"Hello, Natalie, Mr. President." I smiled cautiously at both of them.

He just nodded his head as he always did. Right behind him came Mr. Carter, Christopher's father.

"Hazel, it's not on the schedule, but I'll be spending the morning with Chris and my husband from the office. We're going over a delicate client case." I nodded.

"Oh, that's fine. If you need anything, I'm at your disposal." She ended up asking for her morning coffee. I got up from my chair and prepared a cup for the three of them.

Besides being president, Christopher helped manage the family law firm, and from what Savannah had confided, the Fitzgeralds worked with their companies' stocks, buying and selling, thus increasing their million-dollar income.

It wasn't enough to be the most well-known political family; they had to be smart to always multiply their financial assets.

CHAPTER THIRTY-SEVEN

Hazel

I looked up when Ethan stopped in front of my desk.

"Good morning, Hazel," he greeted me right away.

"Hi, Ethan." I responded politely with a smile.

"How was your weekend?" He always asked these questions as if he wanted to make small talk.

"Couldn't have been better." I shrugged my shoulders.

"Did you bring lunch today, or do you accept an invitation to lunch?" Just as Ethan asked that, the door to Natalie's office opened.

Christopher heard what Ethan said and immediately narrowed his eyes at the man.

"Is there a problem with your desk, Mr. Miller?" Christopher walked slowly toward Ethan.

"No, Mr. Fitzgerald," he hadn't understood that Christopher was angry.

I widened my eyes as I saw the president stop in front of Ethan. Christopher was much taller than him; poor Ethan never had a chance against the president.

"I'll be very clear: stay away from Miss Bellingham. If I see you again or hear that you're circling her, I'll have you fired," he growled in a whisper.

Ethan took a step back, probably not expecting that. You didn't need to be an expert to understand that after Christopher's warning, we were having an affair.

"Yes, sir, understood," obediently Ethan nodded, as if he was bowing his head and submitting like a cornered animal.

Ethan rushed out while I got up from my chair and fixed my gaze on the president, who was taking deep breaths.

"Christopher," I said in reprimand.

But he didn't say anything. He came toward me, grabbed my wrist, and led me to one of the rooms, which should have been his, but was usually empty since he was the president of the country.

He closed the door behind him and locked us inside while his hands held the sides of my face.

"What the hell is that man's problem with you? Is it so hard to keep his distance from you?" he roared, not taking his eyes off mine.

"Christopher, there's no problem," I said, maintaining my calm.

"You are mine, mine... only mine." His lips pressed against mine, and releasing my face, he slid his hand up my skirt, lifting it and pulling me onto his lap.

I couldn't say anything as his lips touched mine with lust. I ran my hand up his neck as the president set me on the mahogany desk, which was bare.

His fingers touched the middle of my legs, brushing over my panties, which were damp at that moment.

"Chris, this is my workplace; what are you doing?" I gasped, my voice breathless.

"I need to fuck you, now, hard, to kill this jealousy that's consuming me from inside." His hands urgently opened his pants, freeing his extremely erect penis.

"Oh, God..." I knew I wanted this, but how would I face Natalie afterward?

Without thinking about the consequences, I just gave in to the lust that consumed me.

"Fuck, it's been so long since I've felt this damn sensation. I feel like I could kill someone just for getting close to the woman who's mine!

You're mine, sweet, daring girl," he grunted, pushing my panties aside and thrusting into me forcefully.

"Chris..." I bit my lip, scratching the back of his neck. "We're just having sex; how can anyone know I'm yours? How can you be jealous of something that isn't even visible to others?"

I tilted my head back as his hand spread out in my hair, pulling it hard.

"Hell! Then be mine, damn it! Make everyone see that you're mine!"

That wasn't his sober side talking. It was as if he were consumed by jealousy, having just seen a man hitting on me. Which was already normal for me, especially when it came to Ethan.

There was no reason for Christopher to be jealous; that man was incredible, so why was he so possessive? I even believed it was a flaw of all the Fitzgeralds.

Without answering his demand, I lost myself in the desire of my body, my legs wrapped around his waist. Christopher thrust forcefully, our lips touching in a lascivious kiss, tongues entwined.

If someone had asked me what I could experience that day, having sex with Christopher in the middle of the office was certainly not one of them.

"Hazel, tell me you're mine," his voice was filled with clear desperation.

"Chris... my president." I sighed as I was filled by his huge member. It was impossible even to speak; he was intense, taking me in a way no one else could. I obviously wanted to be his, but who would guarantee that now that he had had me, he wouldn't want to try other women?

"Answer me, Hazel!!!" he exclaimed, pulling my hair harder.

"Yes, oh... yes, I am yours," I moaned, and even though I tried to hold it in, the moan escaped my mouth. But luckily, Natalie's office wasn't right next door.

Saying that was like surrendering to the peak of my pleasure, gripping the back of his neck as my legs tightened around him, carrying me to the delicious wave of orgasm.

"Fuck!" Christopher roared, holding me and coming deep inside my pussy.

He stayed holding me as my head rested on his hard chest, and his fingers released my hair while his hand, which had been gripping my thigh, now caressed my arm.

"Hell, I lost control," he whispered with his head on mine.

"Does this happen often?" I murmured, trying to find my lost voice.

"Actually, it doesn't happen; I don't claim any woman." I pulled away from him, our eyes meeting.

"Chris, you need to understand that not all the men who talk to me want me in their bed..."

"Yes, not all of them, but that damn Miller does," he growled.

"Well, maybe he does, but you need to trust me. I can handle the men who think they can hit on me." I smiled sideways.

"I lost control." Gradually, he withdrew from me, pulling up his pants. "I can't stand the thought of a man desiring what is mine!"

"Chris." I gasped, not knowing what to say about all this possessiveness. "I think all this is new to me."

"Sorry if I scared you, I promise I'll control myself," he said, helping me get off the desk.

"You came inside me again, I don't use contraceptives, and taking the morning-after pill isn't effective." I sighed as Christopher helped pull down my skirt.

Holding the sides of my face.

"You didn't answer my question; don't think I forgot it," he whispered during a brief kiss.

"Christopher, honey, are you there?" Natalie knocked on the door, calling for her son.

"Yes, mom, I'm on a call, I'll be out soon," he answered his mother without taking his eyes off mine.

"Will you come for lunch with us? Hazel must have gone out for lunch; I didn't find her at her desk."

"Hazel is here with me; she will have lunch with us." I widened my eyes.

"What is my assistant doing with you?" Natalie continued speaking.

"Helping me?" He had that mocking smile on his face.

"Fine, come on then, your father is hungry."

"Christopher, your mother isn't inattentive; she will notice something is going on," I said as the lady walked away from the door.

"I don't care; I want to make sure you're safe and sound having lunch by my side." He winked with a flirtatious look.

"You're impossible, Mr. Fitzgerald." I held his jacket and gave him a kiss on those delicious lips.

"By the way, I want your answer."

"I feel like this is going too fast; we could end up hurting each other," I murmured anxiously.

"Hazel, know that what happened today was just a sample of what I'll do to any man who dares to touch my woman."

"I'm not yours," I said quickly.

"Not yet..."

CHAPTER THIRTY-EIGHT

Hazel

"We'll go in two cars," Natalie declared as we approached the sidewalk.

"I can take my truck," I declared promptly, not wanting to be a burden to them.

"You can go in your car, and I'll accompany Miss Bellingham in mine." Christopher made a face looking at the parking lot and seeing my huge truck there.

"Am I missing something? You two used to hate each other." Natalie looked at us suspiciously.

"Just your impression." Christopher made a gesture with his head, indicating that I should follow him.

Before his mother could ask another question, I followed him. The back door was opened, and I got in, watching the president enter beside me.

I waited for the vehicle to start, following the car in front. Obviously, we were being followed by the Fitzgeralds' security.

"Your mother is suspicious," I said, turning my face.

"Yes, she is," he agreed with me.

"I like your mother a lot; I wouldn't want her to know about this and then get upset if we end up hating each other more than before." I gave a half-smile.

"To end up hating you would take a lot, a lot of effort." Christopher took my hand, his fingers circling mine.

"At first, it was easy to hate me," I joked, since from a sudden hatred, we ended up in the same bed.

"That's because you didn't accept that such a small thing could become my surrender." He winked.

"How was last night?" I abruptly changed the subject.

"Exhausting. We were supposed to end up sleeping together, but Savannah discovered the whole truth, so nothing would stop us from spending the night together, which was a big mistake. I forget that I'm the president of the country, and that requires all my attention." That explained his tired appearance.

"You know, I could have gone along; I would have loved to keep you company." I bit the corner of my lip.

The president caressed my finger.

"Sometimes I forget that I can have someone by my side. The solitary life is somewhat contagious, but it's not something I like. Before I know it, I'm retreating, closing myself off." He seemed lost in his thoughts.

"Chris, you need to understand that I'm very loud; I like chaos." I gave him one of my forced smiles.

"I think I can adapt to that; I'm flexible." The car slowed down as we stopped in front of the restaurant.

We stopped talking as the vehicle came to a halt. The doors opened, and I got out first, meeting Natalie and Carter standing on the sidewalk. We entered the restaurant; I hadn't been there before. Obviously, they had, as no reservation was necessary; the receptionist saw the president at the entrance and immediately found us a table.

Christopher pulled out a chair for me to sit, staying by my side, with Mrs. Natalie in front of me and her husband beside her.

"Do you have any dietary restrictions?" Christopher asked.

"No," I replied, trying not to make any silly jokes.

"We want four of the day's specials and a vintage wine," Christopher didn't even ask what the special was; the waiter just nodded and walked away.

"He didn't ask what the special was," I immediately questioned.

"It's not necessary; we know the chef of this restaurant. He would be offended if we asked." Christopher answered promptly.

"Ronald is a bit egocentric." Natalie smiled delicately.

"The good thing is that he makes delicious dishes," Carter commented.

"Now you can satisfy my curiosity; what did I miss? Are you talking normally?" Natalie looked from me to her son.

"We just decided not to fight anymore," Christopher said.

"He decided; I'm quite determined to keep hating him." I gave a small smile just to provoke him.

"Tell me I can have some hope? Can I still have a chance to have a grandchild?" Natalie's eyes sparkled.

I didn't respond, after all, I liked her a lot. We had a good relationship, talked a lot, and lying to Savannah was painful; now I was lying again. But it wasn't necessary for me to respond, as Christopher said something I wouldn't exactly have said.

"Let's say you have a one percent chance." Obviously, the two in front of us gave a big smile. That's what they wanted.

He could have said 0.01% and Natalie would still remain hopeful; she clung to every small percentage of hope.

"So, are you getting to know each other, I mean in a relationship?" Mr. Carter asked.

"Yes," I answered his question since Christopher had opened up; I wouldn't stay closed off and make it seem like only he wanted this when I did too.

"But how?" Natalie was genuinely interested.

We were interrupted by the wine. The bottle was closed, and it was Christopher who tasted it, approving the essence.

Once approved, he allowed it to be poured into our glasses.

"Now you can start talking; I'm curious," Mrs. Natalie returned to the topic.

"You can't forget, can you, Mom?" Christopher seemed like a little boy talking to his parents; that version of him was incredibly new to me.

"Of course not. I spent months pushing Hazel toward you, and when I lost hope, you came up with this? I was even getting indignant that I was losing to our lawyer, Ethan..."

"We don't need to talk about him," Christopher cut his mother off.

"My son is jealous; our son is jealous." Even that fact made her smile as she looked at her husband.

"There's no reason to be jealous of Ethan; he's just a colleague I'm friendly with." I shrugged, taking a small sip of the wine.

"A work friend I've seen having lunch with you." I turned my face to meet Christopher's eyes.

"I've seen him having lunch with several women, and I'm not jealous." I retorted.

"Oh, really? So, I can have dinner with another woman tonight, and you won't see it as a problem..."

"Of course, I would!" I widened my eyes.

"See, you're jealous," he seemed convinced he had won that one.

"You're crazy. Has anyone ever told you that? And by the way, you're not going to have dinner with anyone. If you're going to poke your nose into every man who comes near me, know that I'll do the same." I turned my face forward proudly.

I met Natalie's eyes; she was smiling like a child in a candy store.

"I always knew that all these arguments were repressed pleasure." She even clapped her hands.

I believed that of all the times I had seen Natalie, this was the happiest I had ever seen her.

Carter was casting that enigmatic look at his son, as if they could communicate just with their eyes.

"I really hope this is something lasting; otherwise, we'll have a little intrigue in our family. We know that even though Hazel is not a Fitzgerald member, we all consider her as one. So take very good care of her, or you'll have to deal with your cousin," the father warned his son.

"I don't need Zachary; I have a gun if he messes up," I joked with them, who were looking at me in amazement.

"Is that really true? Do you have one?" Christopher asked.

"Yes, it's under the seat of my truck. My father would never let us go alone on the road without being safe."

"With a gun? You're safe with a gun?" The president was astonished, and not in a good way.

"I shoot very well." I shrugged casually.

"That doesn't make me feel any better; I don't like knowing you're in that tub, especially with a gun..."

"Any problem with my truck?" I cut him off.

"Everything. It's not safe; you should drive something better. Maybe that's something I can handle..."

"Oh, but you really can't!" I widened my eyes.

"I can, indeed. I've said I take care of what's mine!"

"I'm not yours!"

"Our dishes have arrived," Natalie said a bit louder, interrupting our argument.

"Thank God." I could hear Mr. Carter whisper.

As our dishes were placed in front of us, I felt the president's finger reaching for mine across the table. I pulled them away just to tease him.

CHAPTER THIRTY-NINE

Hazel

I let out a long sigh as I walked out the college door. I would have to call a ride, since my truck decided not to start when I got home after returning from work.

I had to come to the course in a ride share vehicle.

It must be all the bad things Christopher said about my baby. *It was* true that my truck wasn't exactly new, but it still met all my needs.

I pulled my phone out of my pocket when I heard it vibrate. It was a notification from Christopher. After our brief argument in front of his parents, we barely spoke, both irritated, and I wasn't going to be the one to back down.

I opened his notification and read what he had sent:
"*I'm waiting for you in the parking lot.*"
How did he know my truck wasn't working?

With my eyes narrowed, I headed to the parking lot. It wasn't hard to find him; after all, Christopher didn't travel alone, he always had several cars with him.

As I approached, one of the doors was opened for me. Even though I was apprehensive, I entered and saw him sitting there.

Christopher locked his phone and looked up at me. My door was closed, he came toward me, and tried to kiss me, but I deliberately turned my face away.

"I'm sorry," he whispered, brushing his lips against my cheek.

I turned my face away as he reached to his side and picked up a blue rose, the same shade as the one he had given me last time.

"You know how to win a woman over," I whispered, accepting the flower as I brought it to my nose to smell it. "How did you know my truck broke down?"

"Broke down?" His response made it clear he didn't know.

"I thought you knew, since you're here..."

"No, I didn't know, and I'd prefer not to. I have more than enough reasons to hate that bathtub," he retorted, making his usual displeased face when something didn't please him.

"Know that it has never let me down; it's a great companion." A pout formed on my lips.

"Never, huh? And what's today?" Christopher was right about that.

"Damn! You're right." I slumped my shoulders. "But it's the first day."

"Okay, I know," he whispered.

"If you didn't know about my truck, how did you end up here?" I hadn't even asked where we were going.

"I couldn't stop thinking about you for a single minute of my day. I needed to apologize for that brief argument," he whispered, pulling me closer.

"My president, you know how to be persuasive..." I whispered back, amidst the kiss he started as my hand tightened on his thigh.

"What are you doing this weekend?" he asked through the kiss.

"I'm going to Harvard; I've arranged to meet with Scar," I whispered, seeing him pull away, and even with the car in the dim light, he fixed his gaze on me.

"What are you going to do there?" It was clear he was taking on an authoritative stance, wanting to know everything around him.

"Girl stuff? Going to some bar..."

"No, Scarlett doesn't do that kind of thing," he cut me off.

"Who said that?"

"My cousin is too elegant to go to 'bars.'"

"Seriously, Christopher, are you really saying this? What am I then?" I crossed my arms, growing irritated.

"Obviously, you're not a bar girl either, because you're mine," Christopher being his typical controlling self.

"Scarlett is my friend; she needs a shoulder to cry on, and I'm going to comfort her," I was honest.

"What do you mean, what's going on with her?" Christopher suddenly became the concerned cousin, and I might have said too much.

"She just needs..."

"Hazel, speak now!"

"Okay, okay, let's just say she's dealing with unrequited love, her first love, and I'm going to comfort her." I shrugged.

"Who is the guy?"

"That's none of your business, and if anyone finds out, I'll know it was you who talked and I'll never tell you anything again. Scarlett has the right to love, get hurt, try again; stop putting her in a glass bubble," I was firm in my words.

"Does this include men in that shoulder to cry on?" Finally, he seemed to understand and not invade his cousin's life.

"Initially, yes." I pouted.

"No! That's out of the question. Hazel, I can't allow that, for God's sake!" The president raked his hand through his hair roughly.

"But we have nothing. — I rolled my eyes. — We're just going out, it doesn't mean I'm going to be with other men."

"Be my girlfriend, damn it! I don't want to spend my whole day thinking that another man is desiring the woman who is mine," Christopher seemed desperate.

"How can I believe this request? I've never been in a relationship at this level, but isn't there supposed to be feelings involved in a relationship?" I questioned, confused; my fleeting flings couldn't even be called dating.

"But feelings can be involved; as days go by, we can become more serious," he pleaded, caressing the palm of my hand. "Let only our family know; none of my constituents need to know, I know that's your biggest fear."

I bit the corner of my lip.

"Aren't we moving too fast, dating?" I asked apprehensively, afraid of getting hurt.

"Hazel, in these twelve years, there hasn't been a single woman I've shown interest in. I don't want to lose what I have with you; after all, I'm already forty..."

"Your age will never be a problem, but what if you start wanting to be with other women now?" I asked.

"*Baby*, understand, I'm not a man of many, I'm selective, and I want just one woman, and she's right here by my side," he whispered, bringing his lips close to mine.

"Will we spend the night together?" I whispered, asking.

"Yes, I refuse to have you anywhere but in my bed." He bit my lower lip.

"Here's the deal: tonight, let's just spend time together, provided there are no interruptions." I sighed with his new kiss. "We'll have a lot of sex..."

"I need that," he murmured, tightening his hold on my waist.

"Tomorrow when we wake up, I'll give you my answer." I was almost straddling his lap.

"Hell, will I spend a night of torture?"

"Yes, Mr. President... a lot of torture." To tease him, I slid my hand over his member through his pants; as expected, it was erect. "*Mmm*... this is delicious."

"Hazel, we're in the car," he growled in a whisper.

"I can't wait to get to the White House..."

CHAPTER FORTY

Christopher

I ran my hand down her bare back, feeling her skin goosebumps. Hazel snuggled into my chest, and I felt her nails scratching my chest. She was waking up.

I lowered my gaze and saw her hair spread out on my pillow. If there was a more perfect sight than that, I didn't know it.

I heard her phone start to vibrate several times. I stretched out my arms and grabbed the device; Hazel was still too groggy to notice I had taken it. On a whim, I saw my cousin's name and, for that reason, I pulled down the notification bar, after all, we were talking about my cousin.

But maybe I shouldn't have taken that phone because what I read was a complete absurdity, even making my blood boil:

"Hazel, I called him, what a fool I was. I shouldn't have bought that liquor, but seeing that engagement notice from him caught me off guard; I couldn't handle it. I can't be just a small revenge. Malcolm is engaged; he had no right to do this to me, he shouldn't have used me for this petty revenge."

Malcolm? What the hell was this revenge?

Hazel lifted her gaze, probably feeling my chest tense. Our eyes met. She saw the phone in my hand but didn't reach for it. Another person would have snatched it away quickly, but she didn't. It was a sign that she had nothing to hide from me.

"What did you see that made you tense?" she asked with a tense voice.

"Aren't you going to take the phone from my hand?"

"No, I have nothing to hide. If there's something there, it's from before we met." She held onto my chest, sat up in bed, and pulled the blanket over her breasts, covering them.

"My cousin sent you a message." At that moment, she took the device from my hand.

"*Oh*, that definitely wasn't your business, in this case, a problem that shouldn't be shared by me," Hazel was defending my cousin, which any friend would do for another.

She began reading the message and then lifted her eyes towards me. Without waiting for a response, I got out of bed. I was in my underwear, grabbed my phone, and immediately called Zachary.

"Chris, what are you doing?" Hazel said, alarmed.

"Do you really think I'm going to stay quiet knowing that bastard persuaded my cousin into bed and then walked away as if it was nothing? He's messing with the wrong family." At that moment, Zachary answered the call.

"*Calling me at this hour? Did you fall out of bed?*"

"I want you here, now!"

"*What happened, Christopher?*" my cousin immediately realized I wasn't joking.

"Just come, Zachary. I'm going to call William too because he's very much involved in all this." I ended the call.

I called William, who asked if his presence was really necessary. After I confirmed, he arranged for our jet in California. He would come with his wife, son, and my aunt, as they took the opportunity to travel together when needed.

MY PARENTS WERE WITH my uncles, Arnold and Grace, the parents of Zachary and Scarlett. Hazel was also there; after all, my mother was present and said she didn't need to go to the office.

The door opened, and Hazel practically demanded that Scarlett be present, since they were going to talk about my cousin, and it had to be in her presence.

The voices revealed that everyone had arrived at the same time as they entered the private room at the White House. My cousin William, with his wife Zoey, Malcolm's sister, beside him. My uncles, with Aunt Grace hugging Scarlett; everyone treated her like the little princess of the house.

"Why is everyone here?" William asked, placing his baby's car seat on the sofa.

I waited for everyone to greet each other first. My eyes met Hazel's, which still had a hint of anger directed at me. I moved closer to the sofa where my little one was, stopping by her side; it was almost instinctive to stay near her.

"I hope this is very important; you made me leave my house with my baby just days old," William grumbled again.

"Your marriage is the main cause of all this, just like we had a meeting when Zachary showed up with his daughter, and we resolved everything together. I believe this is our concern as well; after all, if someone messes with one of ours, they mess with all of us. If he thinks this was some kind of revenge..."

"Hazel" Scarlett immediately whispered, looking at her friend.

"Sorry, he took my phone this morning" Hazel's voice was choked.

"Cousin, I... I... — Scar lifted her eyes towards me.

"Scarlett, before we lay everything out here, I want your permission." Even though it might be too late, I wanted to know Scar's opinion.

"We're all here now, but know that I don't want any arguments. I'll make the most sensible decision." My cousin lowered her head.

It was clear she was sad; Malcolm had hurt her. He had no right to do that.

"*Damn*, just say it already, what's going on, sister?" Zachary asked, starting to get worried.

"Well... *I... I...* slept with Malcolm..."

"You what?" Zachary roared, my uncles stood up at the same time.

"Let her speak!" Hazel, as always, spoke a little louder; she knew how to take charge of everything. It was as if she had a gift for being by my side; she didn't even seem intimidated by powerful men.

"I spent that time at Malcolm's grandfather's house with Zoey because I wanted to stay close to my friend. I ended up getting close to Malcolm; I was a fool, thinking for a short period of time that he was a good man who wanted something with me. But I found out he only wanted the feeling of revenge." My cousin forced a smile, wiping under her eyes. "Malcolm snubbed me after *well*... after we spent the night together. He said it was just a petty revenge for his own benefit."

My cousin cleared her throat several times, even sniffling through her tears. My aunt Grace, her mother, came closer and hugged her daughter.

"Now do you understand why this concerns you too?" I said, looking at William.

"I'm going to kill that bastard." Zoey immediately grabbed her husband's arm.

"Are you out of your mind? We're talking about my brother. Don't forget he forgave you."

"What a nice fake forgiveness of his, he forgave you because he slept with my cousin." William, irritated, ran his hand through his hair.

"You need to understand that above all else, he's my brother, but Scar is my best friend, and like a sister, I'm on her side. However, let's not get anyone arrested," Zoey asked, going over to her best friend.

"I don't want you to seek revenge; I just want you to do everything possible to keep his path from crossing mine. I ask that you hire some hacker, anyone, to remove everything from my phone, a filter that prevents anything of his from appearing. I simply don't want to hear Malcolm's name again. If you want to help me, do this for me. It hurts to know I was just a revenge. I never want to hear that man's name again." Scarlett pleaded, and even if she had asked for the world, at that moment, we would have found a way to give it to her.

"Yes, my daughter, we will do that," Uncle Arnold took his daughter's side.

"Don't go after him. I want him to think we're so indifferent that we don't care about his presence. I was wrong to call him last night, and that's why I'm going to change my phone, new number, everything to stay away from him."

"We will certainly be very indifferent. With all due respect to you, Zoey, but the Beaumonts have lost all alliance with the Fitzgeralds from today on. Not generalizing, as your parents will always be welcome. But your brother will reap every damned consequence for thinking he can play with our cousin's feelings," I was honest with my thoughts.

"I understand, and I deeply hope Malcolm doesn't take it personally." Zoey looked at her husband.

"My case is different; we went to bed together, and we're together. I do everything to ensure your happiness, unlike your brother, who played with my cousin's feelings."

Everyone agreed with William's words. We would respect my cousin's request and do what she asked.

"Now that we've decided about this, I want to take advantage of the fact that everyone is here," Hazel said loudly, drawing attention to herself.

CHAPTER FORTY-ONE

Hazel

I hadn't responded to Christopher's request, and with everything that happened this morning, we had forgotten about the "dating" topic. I had an answer for him; even though everything was crazy, I wanted to dive into it.

I had always set relationships aside; in fact, I didn't even care about that aspect, so I was going to embark on this craziness.

Even though it was recent, I knew I wanted to dive in without even knowing how to swim.

Everyone was looking at me, waiting to hear what I had to say. Being Zachary's sister-in-law almost made me a member of their family. Since I knew Christopher was eager to tell his family the truth, I started speaking:

"Well." I got up from the sofa where I was sitting and exchanged a quick glance with Christopher. "Chris and I are dating."

I bit the corner of my lip, anxious as I waited to see what they would say.

"Chris, she even used the nickname to call him?" Grace clapped her hands excitedly.

"There's still hope." Natalie joined in with her sister-in-law's enthusiasm.

"Is this serious? Are you dating?" William spoke with a mocking tone.

"Why does it seem so surreal?" Christopher raised his eyebrows, not understanding.

He extended his hand, taking mine and pulling me closer to him.

"We're talking about you, Christopher, the man who lived in eternal mourning for twelve years." William laughed.

"It took twelve years to find this little troublemaker." I felt his lips brushing against my hair.

"You guys seemed to hate each other." Zoey narrowed her eyes, trying to understand what was happening.

"I think all their hatred ended up in sex." William made his joke again.

"Son!" Abigail, William's mother, came over to us and hugged us. "I'm so happy for you, dear."

Christopher's aunt was as radiant as everyone else.

It was as if they were celebrating an engagement, but it was just a relationship.

My sister came over with little Alexis in her arms.

"Can I hold my little niece?" I asked, taking the baby into my arms.

"Sister, can you believe it? We're going to be in the same family." She teased, as if I was about to get married.

"You know this is just a relationship, right?" I looked down at the little one who was bringing her tiny fingers to her mouth.

"Have you noticed the way he looks at you? That man is hopelessly in love with you, and if he doesn't ask you to marry him, I don't know myself." My sister gave one of her enchanting smiles.

"We haven't talked about feelings yet." I declared, taking advantage of the fact that Chris was with the men.

"But to have accepted this relationship means you feel something for him." My sister questioned, making me think about that subject.

I hadn't thought about feelings, but deep down, I knew that if I didn't feel anything, I wouldn't have accepted his request. If I didn't love Christopher, I was on my way to loving him.

Without answering my sister's question, the Fitzgerald ladies approached. Talking openly about feelings wasn't really what I wanted to discuss at that moment.

My niece ended up falling asleep in my arms. I moved closer to her stroller, lifting my gaze when Chris came over.

"You look beautiful holding a baby, you know?" He whispered so as not to wake Alexis.

"Really? I've always wanted to be a mother." His smile faded, looking almost lost in thought.

I got up when Alexis was comfortably settled.

"What's wrong, Chris?" I asked, moving closer to him, lifting my face just enough to look into his eyes.

"Nothing, I just got lost in my thoughts." He pointed to his head.

"Does the topic of pregnancy affect you?" I asked again.

"Actually, I'm scared, scared of losing you, you know, because I lost both once, I was crazy about Anna. And my biggest fear came true when I lost her forever. I don't want the same to happen with you, so every time I'm overprotective, know that it's my dark side speaking louder. I'm afraid of losing you; I don't want the same thing to happen, and if it does, I swear to God I wouldn't be able to handle it. I can't bear to live without you, Hazel." He spoke in that anguished whisper.

"Hey." I held his face. "Nothing is going to happen to me, okay?"

"Anna said the same..."

"Let's make a deal?" He nodded. "I won't mind when you're overprotective. If you feel like you're crossing too many boundaries, I'll let you know. But really, I won't mind."

"Really?"

"Really." I stood on my tiptoes and gave him a lingering kiss on the lips.

"Sorry for always bringing up Anna in your presence; it must not be comfortable." He gave a forced smile.

"Actually, I feel a little jealous." I pouted.

"Jealous?"

"Yes, she will always be in your life. I won't be your first, so..."

"You are my first, the first daring one who took over my thoughts, the only one who tamed me even though you're a little crazy. You know that no one else could achieve what you did."

"What do you mean?"

"In twelve years, all the women I looked at didn't have any sparkle. However, every time I look at you, I see the same sparkle, but even stronger. I feel like I could throw myself in front of a moving car. Never compare yourself to her, as you will always be unique in my life." His thumb caressed my cheek.

"Really?" This time I was the one asking.

"I swear with everything inside me." He pulled me into his arms. "Hazel, nothing compares to the amazing woman you are."

I couldn't help but fall in love with that man. He left me in awe, never saying anything wrong, besides being handsome, charming, polite, and managing to say everything a woman would like to hear.

And it was all completely genuine. Christopher apparently spoke with great sincerity.

"Chris, you're going to make me fall in love." I bit my lip.

"That's the intention." He bit my lip in return.

Our moment of intimacy ended when they noticed we were talking in the corner.

The Fitzgeralds were amazing; I knew they would accept me well. But experiencing it in practice was like stepping into a new family. Even though I already knew them. Christopher's family accepted me for a second time.

CHAPTER FORTY-TWO

Hazel

One month later...

"This is going to be our first public appearance as a couple. Are you sure I look beautiful?" I asked Christopher, who was standing in front of the door to what should be his room but, for the past few weeks, had become more ours, with even a spot for me in his closet.

"Hazel, if there's a way to look less beautiful, I don't know it." He came towards me, stopping in front of me. "You'll be the most beautiful woman at this event."

He leaned down, touching our lips. A slow kiss, nibbling at my lower lip.

"This is a big step, I'm sure, my president." I sighed as he turned me to face the mirror in the room.

"There were never any doubts on my part." He whispered, sliding his hand along my waist.

He was behind me. The burgundy red dress covered my curves in a strapless style, while my loose hair fell over my shoulder, creating a wavy effect.

"My president." I raised my hand and touched his face without turning around.

"My future First Lady." I shook my head with a silly smile.

I turned to face Christopher.

"First Lady?" I narrowed my eyes.

"Yes." He winked mischievously.

In our first month officially dating, many things had happened, like Christopher almost persuading me to move in with him and my father discovering about our relationship through Savannah, who inadvertently mentioned it to them during a call.

Dad initially wanted to come to Washington DC to confront the man who asked for his daughter's hand in dating without his permission. That was until he found out who the man was and, as a good Fitzgerald fan, he could have listened to his fireworks from afar if possible.

"Where's your heel?" He asked, and I looked around, pointing with my finger.

Christopher moved away and grabbed the red pump. He sat on the small bench, resting one of his knees on the ground, which made me smile as he held my ankle and put each heel on my feet.

"Mr. President, at this rate, I'm going to end up falling in love." I repeated what I always said.

"It's hard to change that status." He joked, easily getting up from the floor.

It was obvious that I was already crazy in love with him, but I didn't want to be the first to say it.

"I think we have an event waiting for us." I bit my lip.

"Before that, I have something for you." He went to the bed where there was a small rectangular box.

"Chris" I murmured, knowing it was another one of his gifts.

He returned, opening the box in front of me. Inside was a beautiful necklace with small diamond stones.

"It's beautiful." I whispered, enchanted by the beauty of the jewel. "I'm going to get very spoiled."

"Everything for my woman." He placed the box on the dresser and put the necklace around my neck, which highlighted my exposed bust from the strapless dress.

"It's official, I'm going to become the most pampered woman in the world, even surpassing my sister." I teased, our eyes meeting in the mirror.

I touched the beautiful necklace with the tips of my fingers.

"If I weren't, I wouldn't be doing my job correctly." He kissed my shoulder. "Now, you're ready to go."

He held my fingers, and before leaving the room, I grabbed my small purse, which only had my phone inside.

"Do you know if Malcolm will be there?" I asked, walking down the hallway.

"No, I didn't extend the invitation to the Beaumonts." Christopher spoke seriously.

"Do you think he's starting to notice that he's being boycotted at all events?" We went down a step at a time.

"Yes, his grandfather called me wanting to know if something had happened. Mr. Ralph has always been a good man, with a direct connection to us. For Ralph to call, it means his grandson mentioned something to him."

"And what did you say to him?" I asked curiously.

"I told him to ask his grandson what he did to earn our disdain. His family connection is only with Zoey and William, as she is his sister. With us, there's nothing more, only the professional. I thought we were friends, but out of a petty revenge, he decided to mess with Scar's feelings." All the Fitzgeralds took Scarlett's side.

"Thank you for doing what Scar asked." I smiled at my boyfriend.

"I would love to smash that bastard's face, but I can't. So I'll do what I do best, exclude him from all places that would be good for a possible alliance."

"How vengeful my boyfriend is." I touched his chest as we walked. "That's so sexy... I'm feeling quite wet right now..."

I murmured close to his face. Christopher tried not to smile, but it was impossible to hold back.

"What's the timeframe your gynecologist gave for the contraceptive to take effect?" Christopher asked enthusiastically.

"President, I started taking it a day ago; it will still be a month." I teased.

I had seen a gynecologist because I needed some form of contraception since Christopher kept forgetting to use condoms. The doctor had me take a quick pregnancy test, which came back negative. Seeing that negative result brought me some relief, even though my period still hadn't arrived.

The doctor said that, since the result was negative, I could start taking it even though it wasn't the ideal decision since my period should have started first. But since I was in a hurry, she authorized it.

"If you had started a month ago, we'd be completing the first month by now."

"How was I to know you wouldn't give in to other women?" We exited through the door of the White House.

The cars were all there, many of them waiting for us. Christopher never left without his security detail.

"Baby, how could I give myself to another woman when my body desires only one?" I entered first through the open door.

"I think I'll have plenty of time to get to know your body." My voice had a hint of mockery.

"Is a lifetime a good amount of time?" Christopher was literally the last romantic.

Not even the fact that he had once been in love with another woman and had experienced a great love interfered with what we had. It was as if the past had faded far away. He made no comparisons and made me feel unique and special.

He threw himself into our relationship, being the man I needed in my life.

It was worth not falling in love before, not giving my heart to someone else when he took it with care, embracing me, making me feel unique.

For twelve years he had been celibate, but he hadn't lost the essence of knowing how to handle a woman. He might have been grumpy with others, but with me, it was different, sometimes a bit stubborn, but what can you do, I was stubborn too.

Whoever said that opposites don't attract didn't know us.

CHAPTER FORTY-THREE

Hazel

The car stopped in front of the enormous event, and even before the doors opened, flashes began to come toward the car.

"Wow," I whispered, amazed.

"Are you okay?" Chris stroked my hand.

"Yes." I gave him my best smile, even though I was apprehensive.

"It'll be fine." He brought my hand to his lips and gave it a kiss.

My door was opened, and I extended my hand, holding onto the security guard's. Soon, Christopher appeared at my side, and I felt his fingers on my back.

Thousands of flashes were directed at us, making it difficult to see. This was definitely nothing compared to the last event I attended with Scar.

I just kept my smile on my face, guided by Christopher, not knowing where I was going.

Finally, we entered the enormous ballroom, and I could see again, taking in the incredibly beautiful, luxurious surroundings.

"They say these kinds of parties have the best fundraisers," I whispered next to my boyfriend.

"That's the goal, to raise as much as possible for the children's institute at the orphanage." He winked.

"My boyfriend is a great man." I repeated his gesture, winking and touching the corner of his face, just as a flash went off in our faces.

I turned to see a photographer who had captured our intimate moment.

"Wow," I whispered, amazed.

"Sorry, this will happen more often." Christopher gave me one of his guilty smiles.

"I'm fine, really. It's just new." I looked at the photographer. "Do these photos go up on a website? I'd like this one in particular."

The man looked at me in surprise, as I had made the request and smiled at him kindly.

"I'm from the *Wall Street Journal*." I approached him, extending my hand.

"By the way, I'm Hazel Bellingham." The man blinked several times.

"*Oh*, Kevin Born." He accepted my handshake.

"Will you be the only one photographing tonight?"

"No, but the other journalists are from the *Wall Street Journal*, my colleagues."

"Great." I turned to Christopher, knowing I couldn't give out my number. "Darling, can you give me your assistant's card? I want the photos from the event where we're together, after all, it's our first moment together."

Christopher broke into a wide smile. He approached and handed his card to Kevin.

"Send all the photos to my assistant; my wife wants them." The photographer gladly accepted the card, his eyes shining.

"Yes, Mr. President, it will be an honor."

"Do what you've been asked, and you'll have direct contact with my assistant." That was initially what many journalists would have wanted.

"It will be a great pleasure." The man tucked the card away and moved away from us.

"You know you just got a page all about you, right?" Chris said as soon as we were alone.

"*Oh, no,* that must be really bad." My heart started beating faster, a distressing feeling taking over me.

"My little one, it's not bad; it's good. You were polite to a reporter, you know that besides photographers they are reporters, and generally, people tend to be ignorant with them, but you didn't even know him and were polite." He gently held my chin.

With that fact, I gave him a big smile, trying to calm myself, but it wasn't entirely effective as I still felt a bit confused.

We continued walking through the venue. Christopher seemed to know everyone, and I, by his side, smiled at everyone, even participating in some conversations.

We met up with Zachary and Savannah.

Many politicians were there. Looking around, even though Chris had said Malcolm wouldn't come, I hoped Malcolm wouldn't make a surprise appearance. I was scared of what Zachary and Christopher might do if he showed up.

I positioned myself next to my sister, and we exchanged a quick hug.

"What do you think?" Sav whispered.

"Like a painting on display, look at those women up front." We discreetly glanced at the women who were casting glances at us.

"They're wondering what a shorty like you has to offer to win the heart of the most desired president," my sister teased.

"Coming from the woman who's the same height as me." We shared a restrained laugh.

"You'll get used to it, sister. Many women will look at you with a hint of envy, others will admire you. And that goes for men as well..."

"Men?" I widened my eyes in amazement.

"Yes, trust me, it's all there." My sister held my shoulder.

Zachary placed his hand on his wife's waist, pulling her closer to him. Christopher did the same, and I felt his hand on my back, his firm touch, his large body covering part of mine.

We didn't start a conversation when Chris was called into a circle of politicians, and without removing his hand from my back, he guided me along, as if he were proud to introduce me as his girlfriend. No one made jokes about the president, but I bet many wished they could, because I would have wanted to make several myself.

Everyone respected the president greatly, so they greeted me reservedly.

We returned to Zachary and Savannah's side when Christopher went to the stage to give a speech.

"Don't worry, I'll take care of her, I'll punch anyone who looks at your girl," Zachary joked as I stood by my sister.

"Perfect." Chris moved away with a smile on his lips.

My boyfriend stopped behind the podium, and immediately everyone began to applaud the president's presence.

I was mesmerized by his presence, my eyes fixed on everyone around him.

"Thank you to everyone who is here. Our collector is moving along the side of the hall, and those who wish to make a contribution, please note, it is not necessary to leave your name. Remember, the donation needs to come from the heart..."

He continued with his speech, and all I could do was remain more mesmerized by him. My thoughts drifted, and I blinked several times.

My vision became blurry.

"Sister, are you okay?" Savannah held my wrist.

"*Yes... yes...*" I whispered, even though I wasn't okay.

Soon a new arm wrapped around my waist; I would recognize that arm anywhere.

"What's wrong with her?" Christopher asked, concerned.

"I'm fine..." I whispered, lifting my eyes. How did he get here so quickly?

Wasn't he on stage just now?

"Hazel, my love, come, I'm going to take you out of here." Did he just call me his love?

That was truly experiencing paradise. I was in paradise, living paradise, until suddenly everything just went black.

CHAPTER FORTY-FOUR

Christopher

As if anticipating that reaction, my arms quickly moved under her, and I picked her up into my lap when the little one passed out.

"Hazel" I called her name, exasperated.

Savannah came to my side, touching her sister's face; like me, she was also anxious.

"What happened?" Savannah asked, looking at me. "Did something happen to her, my God, Christopher, is she having some kind of problem?"

"No! She was fine" I roared, turning toward the door. "The hospital is nearby; I'll take her there."

As we passed through, paths were opened for us.

I could hear Zachary and Savannah's footsteps behind me. My cousin must have called my cars, as they were waiting for us outside when we arrived.

"Let's go in the car behind" Savannah said as she headed towards the other car.

At that moment, I didn't care about the flashes directed at us; all I wanted was to get to the hospital.

"Go as fast as you can, run red lights, do whatever is necessary, just get to the hospital quickly" I ordered, my voice strained.

My driver nodded and sped away. I lowered my gaze, my fingers constantly checking her pulse.

A film was playing in my mind. That day when I received the call, my wife being rushed to the hospital, between life and death. Anna arrived alive at the hospital, but the consequences were terrifying; she left me forever.

And now I was rebuilding myself, given a new chance. Hazel was my little angel, the only one who had pulled me from the depths, she couldn't leave me now, this couldn't be her end! *Damn*! What kind of fucked-up fate was this? Was it giving me hope only to take it away?

"Hazel, please don't leave me" I whispered, running my hand over her face. "Don't leave me... irritate me, make all my days chaotic, argue with me..."

I felt my eyes fill with tears. Her hand that was on mine squeezed it gently.

"Hazel?" I called her name.

"Promise?" Her voice was a hoarse whisper.

"*Damn*!" In my relief, I ended up cursing.

She didn't say anything, just slightly opened her eyes, smiling to the side.

Holding her like this in my arms, I realized that I was completely in love with this woman. The fear that gripped me when I thought I might lose her. A tear rolled down my face and fell onto her cheek.

"Are you crying, Mr. President?" Her voice was soft, with that mocking tone.

"I was scared, very scared..." I gasped, seeing her trying to sit up. "Stay lying down, we're almost at the hospital."

"Hospital? I don't need that..."

"You do need it, let's see if it's nothing serious" I was firm in my words.

"I'm better..."

"Hazel Bellingham, nothing you say will change my mind. I was scared, *hell*! I thought I'd never go through this fear again. I can't lose you, understand? I can't lose the reason for my life." I didn't even pay attention to my words, just speaking them as if on autopilot.

"What did you say, Chris?" The little one stayed quiet.

"I said I love you, I love you so much that I'm biased. I've felt this before, but now it's different. It's more intense, *stronger*, it's like I know I could lose you, so I want to savor every second, every moment. I love you, my little wild one." I touched her rosy cheek.

Hazel smiled, rolled her eyes, and passed out again.

"No, no, no!!!" I exclaimed, and fortunately, we stopped right in front of the emergency room at that moment.

I hurriedly got out of the car, running toward the entrance. It was as if everyone was already expecting me; nurses appeared with a stretcher, and I laid her down on it.

"Mr. President, we'll have updates soon" one of the nurses said while others took the stretcher away from me.

I stood there, my feet seeming glued to the ground, the pain taking over me. A strong hand touched my shoulder.

"It will be alright, Chris." I turned to see Zachary.

It felt like a flood of negative emotions overwhelmed me, my body trembled, and when I realized it, my cousin was already pulling me into a hug, and I held him tightly.

Desperate tears consumed me, so many tears, I cried on Zachary's shoulders, fear, terror...

"I can't, I can't lose her... damn it, I love that woman, they can't take away something I love again." I gripped Zach's back.

"You won't lose her, Hazel will be fine" my cousin whispered comforting words.

On my back, I felt Savannah's gentle hand.

"Chris, my sister is strong; she will be okay." It was clear that Savannah was also crying.

"Hazel was fine; she didn't show any signs of being unwell. How did this happen? How did I not notice?" I said, gradually stepping away from my cousin and rubbing my eyes to clear the remnants of tears.

"It's not your fault. It could be some emotional issue; after all, she's dating the president of the country." My cousin put a comforting hand on my shoulder.

"Let's go to the waiting room." Savannah pointed to the chairs nearby.

We nodded and went to that area. Zachary sat next to his wife, but I couldn't sit down without knowing that my little one was somewhere, without having news of her.

I paced back and forth, impatience overtaking me. I looked up and saw my parents coming through the door. Savannah or Zachary should have informed them since I hadn't even had a chance to check my phone.

It wasn't long before the room was filled with all the Fitzgeralds.

"*Hell*, why isn't anyone bringing any information?" I grunted, running my hand aggressively through my hair.

"Calm down, son, they'll bring information soon" Mom spoke calmly.

At that moment, a doctor appeared with a woman who also seemed to be a doctor.

"Family of Miss Bellingham?" he called out.

"I'm her boyfriend" I said, seeing Savannah come to my side.

"I'm her sister." Everyone gathered around me. Hazel was deeply loved by all the Fitzgeralds.

"Hazel arrived unconscious. Some blood tests were done, but initially, we believe it was an emotional issue. Is she going through any problems?"

"Not that I know of. Chris?" Savannah looked at me, wanting to know.

"No, she woke up cheerful; we've been having good days." I frowned, not understanding.

"I'm the obstetrician handling the emergency" the woman spoke. "We believe it might be a symptom related to her pregnancy..."

"What?" I widened my eyes. "Hazel took one of those home pregnancy tests two days ago, but it was negative, and the gynecologist authorized her to start taking birth control."

"Home pregnancy tests can sometimes give false negatives. Miss Bellingham has a high beta HCG level. We did an ultrasound and were able to see the gestational sac, indicating a pregnancy of approximately six weeks..."

"But we haven't been together for six weeks." My blood boiled.

"Calm down, Chris. Gestational age is counted from the last menstrual period, not from conception." Savannah noticed my state of mind.

"So she's pregnant?" I asked, astonished.

"Yes, a twin pregnancy" the obstetrician said, and at that moment, I was the one who almost passed out.

"Is my sister awake?" Savannah asked as she could hear a sniffle, and I knew it was from my mother.

"Yes, Hazel is awake and asking for her sister Savannah and boyfriend Christopher" the doctor responded, and I almost laughed with relief.

Hazel was awake, my Hazel, intact, and pregnant...

CHAPTER FORTY-FIVE

Hazel

How do I tell Christopher about this? I was pregnant. Inside me was growing a baby... two babies...

In my hand was the IV line, through which medication and even saline were flowing.

The doorknob turned, my eyes went to it, my sister walked in, and right behind her was Christopher. A spontaneous smile escaped as soon as I saw them.

"Sister." Savannah ran towards me, throwing herself into my arms.

"Sav" I muttered, feeling the force she applied.

"Oh, sorry." Savannah pulled back, holding my hand.

On the other side of the bed, Christopher took my free hand while his finger caressed my cheek.

"I'll leave you two alone soon." My sister noticed that we wanted to be alone. "I just need to say that I called Dad, and they're on their way."

My sister bit her lip.

"*Oh*, no, Dad is going to freak out." I sighed.

"Sorry, I was a bit desperate..."

"No, it's good that they're coming. After all, I want to meet them. Yes, I already know them, but now they'll be like my in-laws." Chris winked playfully.

"So it's not as bad as it seems, *right*? — My sister gave a sideways smile.

"I guess not." My voice was still weak; sleep was overtaking me.

"*Well*, I'll leave you alone." My sister smiled mischievously. "*Oh*, I'm so happy, I'm going to be an aunt. If you hear fireworks, it's Aunt Natalie setting them off."

She laughed, turned, and went to the door, saying before she left: "Don't get too excited; I'll be back soon. I want to know more about your health." Savannah left the room, leaving me alone with Christopher.

"So you already know." I bit the corner of my lip.

"About the fact that I'll be a father?" Chris caressed my hand.

"Yes." I kept biting the corner of my lip. "Sorry..."

"Are you apologizing for being pregnant?"

"Actually, it's for all of this. I fainted, was rushed to the emergency room, and now I'm pregnant. I can imagine the headline: *President's Crazy Girlfriend Faints.*" I shrugged my shoulders.

"I haven't seen any headlines. Whatever they're saying, I'm not worried at all. My only concern was right here in this bed." Christopher ran his hand through my hair.

"And what about the fact that I'm pregnant?" I made a face, waiting for his response.

"That's definitely the best news I could receive, of course, after knowing that you were okay." He bent down and touched my lip.

"I have a dry mouth" I whispered.

"You're perfect, *Mommy*." He just pulled his face a little away from mine.

"It wasn't supposed to be this way, but I'm going to be a mommy." I placed my hand on the center of my belly.

"I want to do it in the right sequence... or skip one of them." He cleared his throat, focusing on my hand on my belly.

"Skip one of them?" I frowned, not understanding.

"Yes, you'll understand soon." He kissed my lips again.

"What are you planning, Mr. President?"

"You'll find out in due time." He winked, then became serious again. "I was so scared today, scared of losing you..."

"Chris." I raised my hand to touch his hand. "I'm here, I'm fine, we're fine..."

With my other hand, I touched my belly.

"Hazel, can you do a few things for the sake of my mental sanity? Damn, I'm so afraid of losing her, especially now that she's pregnant." He closed his face in a way that was clearly worried.

"Mr. President, you want me to sell my truck, don't you?" I gave him a small smile.

"Yes, that's one of my requests. Another is to get rid of that pistol, and then use one of my drivers. That's *to* start with. I promise I won't be intrusive, but this is a matter of safety..."

"Chris." I lifted my hand to touch his face. "It's okay, I'll talk to Sav about selling the truck. After all, it was hers before it was mine, and I'll give the pistol to Dad so he can take it to Arizona. I'll use your security, but I don't want to stop my life because I want to continue my studies. I want to be a licensed lawyer and also continue being your mother's assistant."

"You're really agreeing to my requests." I nodded my head. "I don't want you to quit your studies, and I'm sure that Mrs. Natalie will love having her daughter-in-law around, especially seeing the whole progression of the pregnancy."

"Your mom must be freaking out." I let out a spontaneous laugh.

"Mom must be changing her will right now." Christopher rolled his eyes affectionately.

"So we've settled everything this quickly? We've agreed on everything, seriously?" I mocked.

"We're starting to understand each other..."

"Compromising." I shrugged my shoulders. "We're good at compromising."

Christopher placed his hand on my belly, over the sheet, as he leaned in and spoke in a whisper to our babies:

"Daddy promises he'll be everything you need. Know that your mother is an amazing woman, the most beautiful I've ever met in my life. She has the most delicate smile, she's a bit crazy, but she will always be our little crazy one." I touched his hair.

"Chris." I felt my eyes fill with tears as all that wave of emotions overwhelmed me. "I think you said you loved me before I fainted again..."

"Yes, I love you, my little wild one." Christopher brought his face closer to mine.

Seeing him so close, his blue eyes, his black hair a bit messy. He was no longer wearing his suit jacket, his tie was loose, with the collar buttons undone.

"If living life intensely means living this way, I think I'm loving it." I whispered, pulling him into a kiss despite our dry lips.

"Now everything makes sense..." his voice trailed off.

"It makes sense?" I asked, not understanding.

"Yes, it was meant to be you, it has always been you, the woman who would be my surrender. All the anger at the beginning, all the ways I sought answers, it was because from the start, it was meant to be you, the answer to my questions."

"Chris..." A tear rolled down my eyes. "I love you, I love you so much... thank you for making all my wishes come true."

"Heavens, I didn't know I needed your love until I had it."

CHAPTER FORTY-SIX

Hazel

I went down the stairs and buttoned the last button on his shirt.

I had been discharged from the hospital the day before. I hadn't even had a chance to spend much time with Christopher; they even threw a party for my arrival at the White House.

Seeing my parents was exhilarating; I was thrilled because being away from them for so many days was very hard.

I walked into the breakfast room, my eyes met those of my boyfriend, and I put my finger to my lips.

I moved towards him. Christopher pulled the chair back, and I sat down between his legs.

"I can't get used to how perfectly my shirts fit you," he whispered, grabbing my waist and sitting me at the table.

My feet were placed on his legs. Christopher was wearing a black shirt and gray sweatpants. I turned and picked up his coffee cup, bringing it to my lips.

"Darling, you'll have many years to get used to it," I whispered, holding the cup's handle.

He reached for the whole grain bread he had prepared and had set aside.

"All the years of our lives." The tips of his fingers grazed my leg.

"You and my dad were chatting a lot yesterday." I pouted.

Christopher moved closer, opening my legs and positioning himself between them.

"Man stuff." I felt his lips touch my leg.

"Aren't you going to say anything?" I sighed, placing the cup on the table.

"No, little troublemaker..."

"Chris." I held his hair as his blue eyes looked up at me. "We need to check with the obstetrician to see if we can have sex with this intensity."

"Not even a little taste now?" Christopher bit my leg.

"My president, you're an insatiable man." I laughed as his hands slid up my legs, tickling me deliciously.

"Totally obsessed with these curves."

Christopher lifted me onto his lap, sat me sideways, and we stayed close, our noses nearly touching.

"You know, I didn't expect to end this year pregnant," I whispered, "but knowing that these babies are from the man I love makes it the best year of my life."

"Definitely the best year of my life, when I was reborn and relived. You made me love, wake up, and sleep every day, like a black-and-white day turning colorful," he murmured, caressing the corner of my face.

"You're perfect, Christopher," I whispered.

I pulled our lips together for a slow kiss, our tongues sliding over each other. A sigh escaped my lips.

"I received the event photos; Sydney sent them to me," I said amidst the kiss. "She said she received them yesterday and immediately forwarded them."

I had a good relationship with his assistant. She seemed highly energetic, an intelligent woman, and, surprisingly, didn't mind being in the president's shadow.

"What did you think of the photos?" he asked, as one of his hands slid down my leg.

"Simply perfect," I whispered with a big smile on my lips.

"It couldn't be less than perfect with you in them." I felt my cheeks flush.

"Are you sure you didn't see any issues with that news report?" I asked, referring to the report with the photo of him crying on Zachary's shoulder.

"At first, I did; it's something intimate of mine, fully exposed for everyone to see." He seemed thoughtful.

"I'm sorry for all the chaos I've caused." I shrugged my shoulders.

They had taken a photo of Christopher crying on Zachary's shoulder, a huge news story, even including a photo of him carrying me in his arms. The headline was *"President of the country dashed off with girlfriend in his arms; could lightning strike twice in the same place?"*

"You'll never be blamed for that; I think I collapsed thinking I might lose you." It was impossible not to smile at the way he spoke.

"I saw many positive comments, many of them praising; maybe Sydney was right..."

"I'm right? Although I'm always right about everything." I widened my eyes as I saw the assistant stopping by the door, luckily sitting sideways on his lap, behaving herself.

"Sydney, there's something called a doorbell," Christopher grumbled as I got up from his lap.

"It's your fault for leaving my entry authorized," she said as she sat in the chair.

"Remind me to revoke the authorization," Christopher grumbled.

"What were you talking about?" Sydney looked up at me. "By the way, you look even more beautiful pregnant."

"My belly isn't even showing yet," Christopher held me by the waist, pulling me closer.

"Believe me, she's looking at your legs," he retorted, narrowing his eyes.

"Your girl is beautiful, but I have a boyfriend." She shrugged, opening her agenda. "What was the subject you were discussing? I want to know why you're right."

"Have they ever told you that you're very curious?" Christopher teased.

"I'm the president's assistant; my job is to be curious." She shrugged.

"We were discussing the fact that the news of Christopher ending up in the headline in Zachary's arms might have been good," I answered, brushing off their jabs.

"It humanized the untouchable president; it was good, showing that it's not just a fleeting romance. It became clear that the most powerful man is in love." Sydney set aside her agenda and picked up a cup. "By the way, am I interrupting anything?"

At that moment, she asked the most obvious question, and it was impossible not to laugh.

"Seriously, Sydney, are you really asking that?" Chris shook his head.

"I'm going to change; I want to take advantage of it being Sunday and spend time with my parents at Zachary and Sav's house." I hopped excitedly. "You should take a break, Sydney; you work too much."

I smiled at the assistant, who returned the smile.

"Our president here demands a lot from me." She half-closed her eyes.

"What would I do without you?" Chris teased.

I bent down, giving my husband a quick peck on the lips as I headed toward the stairs. I was excited; my parents were in town, my family united. I really wished they could live closer to us.

But those were the consequences of adult life, and I loved being with my new family too.

CHAPTER FORTY-SEVEN

Christopher

"Christopher, where are we? I can hear the sound of the sea." She moved her hands, trying to feel something.

I stopped in front of the dock; my family's boat was there. I decided to bring Hazel to our house in Hampton. We would spend the weekend there because I had a real reason for bringing her.

"We've arrived, Miss Curious." I put my hand behind her head, removing the blindfold.

Hazel looked around, her eyes sparkling as I stood by her side.

"A boat?" She turned around, curious.

"On our first day in Hampton, you asked me to take you for a boat ride, and being the arrogant guy I am, I refused, so I decided to bring you out today." I ran my hand down her back.

"Are you kidding me?" My little one jumped up, clapping her hands.

"Come on, my excited lady." Hazel took my hand and, with my help, got onto the boat.

"Wow, this is huge, how do I get used to the fact that my boyfriend has a boat?" she continued enthusiastically. "Do you know how to drive this thing?"

"Yes, I got my license a few years ago," I declared, enjoying her admiration.

"So it's just you and me then?" If there's something I loved, it was watching her.

"Yes, just the two of us." I held her hand. "I'll show you the boat's rooms."

"Rooms?" She let out an excited squeal.

We went inside, into the kitchen, and then down to the lower deck. There was a bedroom, bathroom, and a small living room. I crossed my arms, simply watching her move from one room to another.

"Christopher, we need to spend a night here, seriously, it's beautiful." She stopped in front of me.

"Yes, we'll come on a day with more time; we can spend a night here." I winked, lowering my face to give her a long kiss on the lips.

I took her hand, led her upstairs, and we went to the cabin. Without touching anything, she looked at all the controls.

"Do you want to be my co-pilot?" She looked at me and nodded. "First, let's lift the anchor."

"Just like in the movies? Good thing you're strong." I laughed loudly.

"No, my love, it's just a button."

"No ropes, no boyfriend sweating like a pirate?" Hazel made one of her jokes.

"I'm not the *pirate* type." I narrowed my eyebrows.

"What a shame." She shrugged dramatically.

Following my instructions, we started the boat. Hazel just stayed by my side while I drove, and when we reached open water, I looked to the side, taking her hand.

"Come here." I placed her in front of me.

"Oh, I'm so scared." Hazel exhaled excitedly. "A fear, but a joyful one."

"Yes, I get it, perfect definition—*fear of joy*." I shook my head.

I held her hand from above, guiding her through the open sea, my body pressing against hers.

"Christopher, this is amazing, how do I get a license to drive a boat?" She lifted her face.

"We can talk about that after our kids are born." She nodded enthusiastically. "Let's stop soon, okay?"

"Yes, good thing I'm wearing a bikini underneath; mommy's going to show off this body." She gave a little shake to tease me.

"Mommy can only do that for daddy here." I lowered my face, kissing her neck.

Her giggle made me smile. We reached the point indicated on the GPS, and I anchored the boat there.

"I'm going outside," she said.

I watched her from the cabin. Hazel took off her dress, wearing only her black bikini; she didn't even have a belly yet, but her breasts had grown, becoming fuller.

Slowly, I left the cabin. Hazel looked up at me, her hair flying in the wind, the most beautiful sight I had ever seen.

"Any problem, my president?" I continued walking towards her.

"I never get tired of looking at the beautiful woman who will be the mother of my children." I stopped in front of her, took her by the waist; her belly hadn't grown, but it was firmer, somewhat hard, clearly showing that our children were growing there, whether they were sons or daughters.

"Chris" she whispered, holding onto my shoulder. "I loved the surprise."

"I brought you here for a reason." I removed my hand from her waist, reached into my pocket, and pulled out a small velvet box.

I knelt in front of her.

"Oh, my God." Hazel put her hands to her mouth.

"For years, I thought I would spend the rest of my life alone. Hopeless, a man merely surviving one day at a time. Our first moment together was a huge shock. How could that sharp-tongued girl affect me? Me, a man used to everything in its place." I let out a weak laugh. "Hazel, I hated you, but I hated you because I knew deep down I desired you, even without knowing, without realizing it, my body was already begging for yours, until it took over my mind, making me think only of the most daring woman I had ever met. If that wasn't enough, my body, my mind, ended up claiming my heart, taking all its pieces, putting them together and making me yours. *Only yours...*"

I paused, holding her hand, and opened the small box to reveal the engagement ring.

"I had a love in my life, a past love, something I thought I would never get over, but then you came along and made me realize that a man can, indeed, have the chance to love a second time. A stronger, more intense love. Everything I went through was worth it, if in the end, it was to stand by your side." I kissed the palm of her hand. "My sweet, smart, and daring woman, will you accept to be my wife, will you marry me? Make me the happiest man in the world?"

Tears were streaming down her face, and she was even sniffling.

"Christopher, my beautiful and perfect president, I accept to be yours, of course, I want to be your wife, to become the first lady of the most powerful man." She slid the ring onto her finger.

I stood up, holding her in my arms, spinning her around in the air, and listening to her laughter that took over.

"I love you, Christopher Fitzgerald" she shouted loudly, and there I felt that she was my perfect woman.

Hazel would never be the second choice; she would be the first. Anna was a beautiful past, but she remained in the past. A beautiful memory, but my love for Hazel was unlike anything I had ever felt in this life.

I loved her, loved her with everything that was inside me. A crazy, intense, and intriguing love, never knowing what to expect from her, a surprise every day.

EPILOGUE ONE

Hazel

Five months later...

"One... two... three..." I counted along with my bridesmaids.

I tossed the bouquet of flowers over my shoulder, then turned around to see Scarlett holding the bouquet with wide eyes.

My new cousin almost tossed the bouquet back.

"No tossing it again," I shouted to her.

"Do you think this might bring me luck?" Scarlett joked.

"Well, I caught Savannah's bouquet and got married." Zoey laughed and let out an excited squeal.

"I caught Zoey's bouquet and got married," I said, exchanging a look with Zoey.

"Oh, dear, it's cursed." Scar only didn't toss the bouquet because she was too polite to do so.

Scarlett had been improving every day; it had been tough, and she even needed psychiatric treatment. Now, in addition to being friends, we were cousins. Malcolm had never appeared in her life again, and even at Christopher's and Malcolm's first meeting, I had to stay in front of my fiancé.

Malcolm wasn't foolish enough to ask what the problem was but was smart enough to realize that all the Fitzgeralds already knew the truth, with Zoey saying she wouldn't tell him since she was angry with her brother for what he did to her best friend.

The highlight was learning that he had gotten married and apparently didn't appear at many events with his beautiful Victoria's Secret model wife.

Scarlett had gotten over that marriage well, even saying it was good that he had moved on, a sign that it was nothing more than a silly and forgotten revenge.

"Can I know what world that head of yours is in?" Christopher's whisper made my body shiver.

"Just looking at how many amazing people I have by my side." I turned my face, feeling Chris's hand on my belly.

My parents approached, Mom with tears in her eyes; I could even swear she had spent the whole wedding crying.

"My baby is going to be a mommy now." Dad hugged me.

Christopher passed by my mother, touching her shoulder.

"Your baby is going to have a baby," I teased, stepping away from him with a big smile on my lips. "I'm so happy to see you here..."

My dad brushed his hand on my cheek, wiping my tears.

"These little ones make mommy emotional." I touched my belly.

"Speaking of which, the truck is now with your cousin." I hadn't even sold my truck, returning it to my dad, asking him to give it to one of my cousins.

"Glad it's useful to someone." Christopher hugged me at the waist.

"Honey, you know that if these little ones give any sign of coming early, call me immediately." Mom touched my belly affectionately.

"I will, Mom, I'll call." Savannah approached with Zachary by her side.

"At least one of my daughters remembers her mother." Mom made a dramatic pout with her lip.

"Mom, I promise that when Matthew and Michael are born, I'll slow down; for now, I want to study, intern..."

"And I thought she'd stop. She didn't stop even as a child, let alone now that she's pregnant." My dad's voice was full of affection.

"I do try to make her stop, Peter, but this little one is adamant." Christopher hugged me from behind.

"I know exactly how that is, she inherited all my temper, while Savannah is calm like her mother." Dad was the silliest man in the world, going around telling everyone that his daughters had married the President and the Vice President.

"So, I hit the jackpot." Zachary joked.

"Not at all," Christopher retorted. "Hazel is my force of nature, the joy of my days, there's not a calm day in that White House. I wouldn't trade her for all the calm in the world."

I looked up and exchanged a quick kiss with my husband.

"I see I can sleep easy, my daughters are with great men." Dad smiled proudly.

"Look, Peter, I didn't think it was fair when I met you because I was threatened, but Christopher didn't go through the same thing." Zach teased; he had a great relationship with my parents.

"I couldn't threaten the President, and well, I know the Fitzgeralds' character; I already had one as a son-in-law." Dad shrugged.

"Was that a compliment, father-in-law?" Zachary approached Dad and gave him a hug.

I shook my head, laughing at the situation. I lowered my gaze and saw his large hand covering my belly over the dress.

"Come with me," he whispered in my ear.

Linking our fingers, we walked to one side of the hall, where there were some chairs for resting.

My obstetrician had set the limit for us to get married by six months of pregnancy; after that, it would be too risky.

My husband sat in the chair and pulled me onto his lap, where I sat sideways, stretching my legs.

"My legs are killing me," I whispered, panting.

"Are these two making Mommy's belly heavy?" Chris hugged me at the waist.

"These two are going to drive their parents crazy with how much they move in my belly." I lovingly ran my hand over his.

There, were our wedding rings. Now I was a married woman, my husband was the President of the country, and it felt like I was born for this. To be by the side of the most powerful man. I thought I wouldn't be able to handle it, that I couldn't meet the voters' expectations.

But everything about me was positive. Christopher went from a reclusive widower to a charming fiancé, we made headlines in many newspapers, and all of them were about Chris being attentive, helping me with something, in his way, always romantic.

"Your father mentioned your pistol to me." He pursed his lips. "He said he would talk to you, but I don't know if he had the chance."

"No, he didn't talk," I replied, waiting for him to explain what it was about.

"Well, he said that your pistol is in his safe and that he'll keep it for our children. I didn't say anything, but I don't like that idea." Christopher hated the fact of having a pistol.

"Honey, can we save the freak-out for when our boys are older?" I touched his face.

"As long as that thing doesn't end up back in your possession, I'm fine with it." He kissed the tip of my nose.

Christopher was a thoughtful fiancé, which he considered a flaw — his obsessive need for control, always being protective — but to me, it became a minor detail.

I loved him completely, all his flaws and qualities, even when he acted with his uncontrolled jealousy, I loved him even more. Living with Christopher was like having an adventure every day, and the fact that we were different was what drove our relationship to be hotter and more intense.

Loving Christopher Fitzgerald was the sweetest madness I've ever committed in my life.

EPILOGUE TWO

Christopher

Ten years later...

"Dad, are we going to stop by Mommy's office?" Michael asked as I drove.

"Yes, Mommy's car is at the inspection, so we'll stop by to pick her up," I said through the rearview mirror, seeing Michael's smile.

Mitch was very attached to Hazel, while Matthew was my little shadow, as if each one had picked their side. But deep down, they were always united.

"Dad, did Uncle Zachary say anything about that new law contract?" Matthew knew everything about the world of politics.

I had just picked them up from school; usually, our driver would pick them up, but since it was my mother's birthday, I left work early to get them.

My mother would never let one of her birthdays pass without her grandchildren. She was more lenient with them than she had ever been with me in my entire life.

I signaled and stopped the car in front of my wife's law office.

It had been two years since we moved to New York, my second term as President had ended, and all I wanted was to be away from politics, to enjoy my children, and pass the baton to my cousin.

Zachary was in his first term as President. He was a good president, as all the Fitzgeralds were born for it.

I had stayed away from politics for a whole year, living only for my children and my wife, until my party made me an offer to run for Governor of New York.

It was as if duty was calling me. Being a governor didn't involve even half the responsibilities that being a president did.

I had achieved my life's goals, won every battle, fulfilled my objectives, and leading my country was one of them. Now my only duty was to be with them, my children, my wife, and still be able to work in what I loved to do.

A smile spread across my lips when she appeared. Hazel was wearing one of her typical pencil skirts, a loose shirt, and, in a delicate way, walked gracefully in her high heels.

Over the years, Hazel changed. The woman who used to wear boots often now wore heels more frequently. I even told her I didn't mind seeing her in heels. But she ended up changing, saying she wouldn't give up her boots, even though she wore heels more often, and occasionally showed up in one of her boots.

"Hello, men of my life," she said with all her enthusiasm as she got into the car.

"My queen," I greeted her, bringing my face close to hers, giving her a lingering kiss. "How was your day?"

Even though we talked throughout the day, I liked to know.

"Well, actually very well. No difficult cases." Hazel turned to our children, who were leaning in to hug their mother.

Our boys were identical twins, which at first was quite challenging; we even had to use ankle bracelets to tell them apart. Their hair was black like mine, and the only difference was that they had inherited my mother's dark eyes. Otherwise, they looked just like me, which, in a way, made Hazel indignant, as she said she had only served as an incubator.

"And you, my boys?" she asked our children.

"Nothing new, Mom. Matthew is the best at soccer, left a weakling eating dust." Through the rearview mirror, I saw my son proudly talking about his brother.

"Michael said he won several chess games even against older kids" it was amazing how one spoke so highly of the other.

"My boys are the best." Hazel clapped her hands, excited.

"Mom, did we get that thing Grandma asked for?" Michael, being a good grandson, asked.

"Yes, dear," Hazel replied to our boy.

My wife had taken over my family's offices. She was my mother's pride, who literally saw her as a daughter. Mom taught Hazel everything she knew, and the two of them were not just mother-in-law and daughter-in-law but best friends.

I drove into my parents' condominium; they had moved to New York to be close to their grandchildren and to follow their growth up close.

Slowing down, I pulled over. I turned off the car, and before I knew it, our children were already jumping out of the car, running towards the house.

"They love their grandparents," Hazel whispered affectionately.

"How can they not? My parents indulge their every wish; they literally spoil their grandchildren." I rolled my eyes.

"Let them. Your mother spent years thinking she wouldn't be a grandmother, so now she cherishes every minute." We opened the car door, and I quickly reached her side, holding her hand to help her out.

"I don't think even I believed I would have all of this," I whispered, kissing the top of my girl's head.

"Chris, you know you already have my heart; there's no need for you to be this perfect man," she teased.

"You know you will always be my perfect woman; I'll never tire of pampering you." She gave me a charming smile.

"Am I perfect for driving you crazy?"

"I never thought I'd be so happy to be driven crazy." I burst out laughing with her.

Living with Hazel was exactly what I had always thought it would be—each day a surprise, never telling me what I wanted to hear, always honest and saying what I needed. Hazel had me in the palm of her hand; my girl would always be the one who won my heart, pulled me from the depths of despair, showed me what happiness was, gave me our children, and I had no other way to thank her than by loving her with everything that was within me.

I made the mistake of underestimating her many times in my life, but from that mistake, I realized she was the exact woman for me.

Hazel was so perfect that she accepted me with all my flaws. I loved that woman and knew from the bottom of my heart that she would be the only woman I would love until my last breath.

THE END.

Did you love *When Tornadoes Collide*? Then you should read *The Senator's Bargain* by Amara Holt!

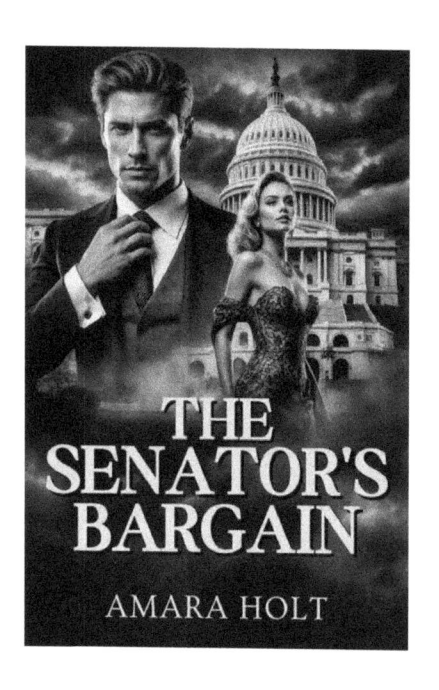

The Senator's Bargain

Power. Control. **Deception**. Richard has it all. As one of New York's most **influential** senators, he's ruthless in his pursuit of the presidency. But when his political ambitions demand a picture-perfect wife, Richard strikes a cold deal: a **marriage contract** with no strings attached, no love involved.

Isabelle, the illegitimate daughter of a failing businessman, has only one priority—**protecting** her little sister. Desperate and cornered by her family's financial ruin, she's forced into an agreement that will change her life forever: marrying a man who views her as nothing more than a pawn in his game.

But as the icy walls between them begin to melt, **forbidden passion** ignites. What started as a calculated arrangement turns into an overwhelming desire that neither Richard nor Isabelle can deny. Yet, when dangerous **secrets** emerge, alliances are shattered, and Richard's trust in Isabelle is broken. He despises her, not knowing she holds a secret that could turn his world upside down—**a future heir.**

In a world where power comes before love and **betrayal** is a constant threat, can Richard and Isabelle's love survive the darkness that threatens to destroy them both?

The Senator's Bargain is a gripping romance filled with intense chemistry, **unexpected twists**, and a love that must overcome the ultimate test. Perfect for fans of age-gap romance, enemies-to-lovers, and high-stakes political drama. Will their bargain lead to heartbreak or happily ever after? Read now to find out.

About the Author

Amara Holt is a storyteller whose novels immerse readers in a whirlwind of suspense, action, romance and adventure. With a keen eye for detail and a talent for crafting intricate plots, Amara captivates her audience with every twist and turn. Her compelling characters and atmospheric settings transport readers to thrilling worlds where danger lurks around every corner.